PENGUIN BOOKS

HOTEL WORLD

'A profoundly moving and life-affirming book' *List*

'A writer of incredible inventiveness, versatility and uniqueness. *Hotel World* is everything a novel should be: disturbing, comforting, funny, challenging, sad, rude, beautiful. A brave, brilliant and breathtaking book' Maggie O'Farrell, *Independent on Sunday*

'A greatly appealing read and a remarkable novel' *Washington Post*

'Smith is an author of rare skill who balances light-footed humour with a genuine profundity and writes with such imaginative flair it renews your faith in the power of fiction' *Metro*

'Haunting and acute . . . invigoratingly sharp writing' *New Statesman*

'Smith's powerful prose transforms these half-lives into miniature epiphanies, subtly working them together into a whole that is full of gaps and puzzles, but never lacking in warmth or humour . . . a rewarding read' *Sunday Times*

'A frighteningly good novel about the persistence of love' *Face*

'Ambitious, disturbing and immensely affecting . . . Rich in finely wrought, evocative detail . . . This is an exceptional novel about people's inescapable inability to divest themselves of the troubling aspects of themselves and their lives' *Big Issue*

'Playful, intelligent writing, but with feeling too' *Esquire*

'Smith's writing is poetic and combines deep compassion and searing judgement about how we humans struggle through life' *Diva*

ali smith

hotel world

PENGUIN BOOKS

PENGUIN BOOKS

Published by the Penguin Group
Penguin Books Ltd, 80 Strand, London WC2R 0RL, England
Penguin Putnam Inc., 375 Hudson Street, New York, New York 10014, USA
Penguin Books Australia Ltd, 250 Camberwell Road, Camberwell, Victoria 3124, Australia
Penguin Books Canada Ltd, 10 Alcorn Avenue, Toronto, Ontario, Canada M4V 3B2
Penguin Books India (P) Ltd, 11 Community Centre, Panchsheel Park, New Delhi – 110 017, India
Penguin Books (NZ) Ltd, Cnr Rosedale and Airborne Roads, Albany, Auckland, New Zealand
Penguin Books (South Africa) (Pty) Ltd, 24 Sturdee Avenue, Rosebank 2196, South Africa

Penguin Books Ltd, Registered Offices: 80 Strand, London WC2R 0RL, England

www.penguin.com

First published by Hamish Hamilton 2001
Published in Penguin Books 2002
9

Set in PostScript Monotype Sabon
Printed in England by Clays Ltd, St Ives plc

acknowledgements and thanks

thanks to the Royal Literary Fund
for their kind help during
the writing of this novel.

thank you, Simon, and thank you, David.

thank you, Philippa, Angus, Kate,
Frances, Xandra, Kasia and Sylvia.

thank you, Becky.

thank you, Donald.

thank you, Sarah.

extract from Edwin Muir's 'The Child Dying' reproduced
by kind permission of Faber and Faber.

all efforts have been made to contact holders of copyright;
in the event of any inadvertent omission, please contact
the publisher.

to

Daphne Wood
for her generosity

Andrew & Sheena Smith
for their kindness

Sarah Wood
for all the world

Remember you must die.
Muriel Spark

Energy is eternal delight
William Blake

Unfriendly, friendly universe,
I pack your stars into my purse
And bid you, bid you so farewell.
That I can leave you, quite go out,
Go out, go out beyond all doubt,
My father says, is the miracle.
Edwin Muir

Traditional religions emphasize constancy,
the Modernists with their mechanistic
models emphasize predictability, but the
cosmos is much more dynamic than either
a pre-designed world or a dead machine . . .
each jump is a great mystery.
Charles Jencks

The fall occurs at dawn.
Albert Camus

past

Woooooooo-

hooooooo what a fall what a soar what a plummet what a dash into dark into light what a plunge what a glide thud crash what a drop what a rush what a swoop what a fright what a mad hushed skirl what a smash mush mash-up broke and gashed what a heart in my mouth what an end.

What a life.

What a time.

What I felt. Then. Gone.

Here's the story; it starts at the end. It was the height of the summer when I fell; the leaves were on the trees. Now it's the deep of the winter (the leaves fell off long ago) and this is it, my last night, and tonight what I want more than anything in the world is to have a stone in my shoe. To be walking along the pavement here outside the hotel and to feel a stone rattling about in my shoe as I walk, a small sharp stone, so that it jags into different parts of the sole and hurts just enough to be pleasure, like scratching an itch. Imagine an itch. Imagine a foot, and a pavement beneath it, and a stone, and pressing the stone with my whole weight hard into the skin of the sole, or against the bones of the bigger toes, or the smaller toes, or the inside

3

curve of the foot, or the heel, or the small ball of muscle
that keeps a body upright and balanced and moving
across the breathtaking still-hard surface of the world.

Because now that my breath, you might say, has been
taken I miss such itching detail all the time. I don't want
anything but it. I worry endlessly at detail that would
never have concerned me, not even for a moment of when
I was still alive. For example, just for peace of mind, my
fall. I would like very much to know how long it took,
how long exactly, and I'd do it again in a minute given the
chance, the gift of a chance, the chance of a living minute,
sixty whole seconds, so many. I'd do it given only a
fraction of that with my full weight behind me again if I
could (and this time I'd throw myself willingly down it
wooo-

hooooo and this time I'd count as I went, one elephant
two eleph-ahh) if I could feel it again, how I hit it, the
basement, from four floors up, from toe to head, dead.
Dead leg. Dead arm. Dead hand. Dead eye. Dead I, four
floors between me and the world, that's all it took to take
me, that's the measure of it, the length and death of it,
the short goodb—.

Quite tall roomy floors, quite quality floors. Nobody
could say I didn't have a classy passage out; the rooms
very newly and tastefully furnished with good hard
expensive beds and corniced high ceilings on the first
and second, and a wide grand stairwell I fell parallel to
down the back of. Twenty-one steps between each floor
and sixteen down to the basement; I fell them all. Quite

4

substantial space from each thick carpet above to each thick carpet below though the basement is stone (I remember it, hard) and the drop was short, less than one complete glorious second per floor I estimate now so long after the event, descent, end. It was something fine. The fall. The feeling. The one-off rough-up; the flight to the bitter end, all the way down to the biting of dust.

A mouthful of dust would be something. You could gather it any time, couldn't you, any time you like, from the corners of rooms, the underneaths of beds, the tops of doors. The rolled-up hairs and dried stuff and specks of what-once-was-skin, all the glamorous leavings of breathing creatures ground down to essence and glued together with the used-up leftover webs and the flakes of a moth, the see-through flakes of a bluebottle's dismantled wing. You could easily (for you can do such a thing whenever you choose, if you want to) smear your hand with dust, roll dust's precious little between a finger and a thumb and watch it stencil into your fingerprint, yours, unique, nobody else's. And then you could lick it off; I could lick it off with my tongue, if I had a tongue again, if my tongue was wet, and I could taste it for what it is. Beautiful dirt, grey and vintage, the grime left by life, sticking to the bony roof of a mouth and tasting of next to nothing, which is always better than nothing.

I would give anything to taste. To taste just dust.

Because now that I'm nearly gone, I'm more here than I ever was. Now that I'm nothing but air, all I want is to breathe it. Now that I'm silent forever, haha, it's all

5

words words words with me. Now that I can't just reach out and touch, it's all I want, is to.

This is how it ended. I climbed into the, the. The lift for dishes, very small room waiting suspended above a shaft of nothing, I forget the word, it has its own name. Its walls, ceiling and floor were all silver-coloured metal. We were on the top floor, the third; it used to be the servants' quarters two hundred years ago when the house had servants in it, and after that the house was a brothel and up there was where the cheap girls, the more diseased or aging girls, were put to sell their wares, and now that it's a hotel and each room costs money every night the smaller rooms still cost a little less because the ceilings are closer to touching their floors up at the top of the house. I took the dishes out and put them on the carpet. I was careful not to spill anything. It was only my second night. I was being good. I climbed in, to prove I could; I curled like a snail in a shell with my neck and the back of my head crammed in, pressed hard right up against the metal roof, my face between my arms, my chest between my thighs. I made a perfect circle and the room swayed, the cord snapped, the room fell wooo-

hooooo and broke on the ground, I broke too. The ceiling came down, the floor came up to meet me. My back broke, my neck broke, my face broke, my head broke. The cage round my heart broke open and my heart came out. I think it was my heart. It broke out of my chest and it jammed into my mouth. This is how it began. For the first time (too late) I knew how my heart tasted.

I have been missing the having a heart. I miss the noise
it used to make, the way it could shift warmth round, the
way it could keep me awake. I go from room to room
here and see beds wrecked after love and sleep, then beds
cleaned and ready, waiting again for bodies to slide into
them; crisp sheets folded down, beds with their mouths
open saying *welcome, hurry up, get in, sleep is coming.*
The beds are so inviting. They open their mouths all over
the hotel every night for the bodies which slip into them
with each other or alone; all the people with their beating
hearts, sliding into spaces left empty for them by other
people gone now to God knows where, who warmed the
same spaces up only hours before.

I have been trying to remember what it was like, to
sleep knowing you would wake up. I have been
monitoring them closely, the bodies, and seeing what their
hearts let them do. I have been watching them sleep
afterwards; I have sat at the ends of satisfied beds,
dissatisfied beds, snoring, oblivious, insomniac beds, the
beds of people who sensed no one there, no one else in the
room but them.

Hurry up. Sleep is coming. The colours are going. I saw
that the traffic was colourless today, the whole winter
street was faded, left out in the wind and the sun for too
long. Today even the sun was colourless, and the sky. I
know what this means. I saw the places where green used
to be. I saw almost no reds, and no blues at all. I will miss
red. I will miss blue and green. I will miss the shapes of
women and men. I will miss the smell of my own feet in

summer. I will miss smell. My feet. Summer. Buildings
and the way they have windows. The bright packaging
round foods. Small coins that are not worth much, the
weight of them in a pocket or a hand. I will miss hearing
a song or a voice come out of a radio. Seeing fires. Seeing
grass. Seeing birds. Their wings. Their beady   . The
things they see with. The things we see with, two of them,
stuck in a face above a nose. The word's gone. I had it a
moment ago. In birds they're black and like beads. In
people they're small holes surrounded in colour: blue,
green or brown. Sometimes they can be grey, grey is also
a colour. I will miss seeing. I will miss my fall that
ruined me, that made me wooo-

hooooo I am today. What a fuck, for always, for ever
and ever world-without-end with an end after all, amen.
I'd do it again and again. I go every night since I fell last
summer (my last) up to the top floor, and though the lift is
gone now, to God knows where, removed out of
something akin to good taste (notorious, a tragedy, not-
spoken-about, a shadow-story, my dying got into the
papers one day and blew away the next, a hotel has to
make a living), the shaft is still there suspended behind
the stairwell with its grave promise from up all the way to
down, and I throw myself over and it's all I can do, hover
in the hollow, settle to the ground like boring snow. Or if
I launch myself in, make the special effort to fly down fast
to hit the stone, I go straight through it as if the stone is
water, or I'm a hot blade and the stone is butter. I can
make no dent in anything. I have nothing left to break.

Imagine diving into water, water breaking round your shoulders to make room for you in it. Imagine hot or cold. Imagine cold butter disappearing into heated-up bread, gold on its surface, going. There is a word for heated-up bread. I know it. I knew it. No, it's gone.

Here's the story. When I hit the basement whoo I was broke apart, flaked away off the top of me like the points of flame flake off the top of a fire. I went to the funeral to see who I'd been. It was a bit gloomy. It was a cold day in June; the people had coats on. Actually it is very nice, where they buried her. Birds sing in its trees, and the sound of far-away traffic; I could hear the full range of sounds then. Now the birds are far away, and there is almost no traffic noise. I visit quite often. It's winter now. They've put up a stone with her name and her dates and an oval photograph on it. It hasn't faded yet. It will, in time; it gets the late afternoon sun. Other stones have this too, the same kind of photograph, and the rain gets in and as the seasons move round the stones, heating them up and cooling them down, condensation comes and goes inside the glass over the pictures. That small boy with the school cap on, way across the moundy grass; that elderly lady, beloved wife; that young man in his best suit twenty-five years out of fashion; all still breathing behind their glass. I hope ours will do that breathing thing too. Hers.

Under the ground, in the cold, in the rich small smells of soil and wood and dampening varnish, so many exciting things are happening to her now. Maybe the earnest ticklish mouths of worms; anything. We were a girl, we

9

died young; the opposite of old, we died it. We had a name and nineteen summers; it says as much on the stone. Hers/mine. She/I. Knock knock. Wooo-

hoooo's there? Me. You wooo-

hoooo? You-hoo yourself. Someone has cut the photograph of her so it will fit in. I can see the tremor of careful scissors round the edge of her head. A girl's head, dark hair to the shoulders. Closed and smiling mouth. Bright and shy, the things she saw with. They once were greenish blue. The head in the glass oval is the same one in the frames in the different rooms of the house, one in the front room, one in the parents' room, one in the hall. I chose the saddest people and I followed them to see where we'd lived. They seemed vaguely familiar. They sat at the front in the church. I couldn't be sure. I had to guess. I thought they were ours, the people, and I was right. After the funeral we went home. The house is small; it has no upstairs, no place for a good fall. A chair in that house can take up almost one whole wall. A couch and two chairs fill a room so there is hardly any place for the legs of the people sitting.

A dog was barking at me two houses away. A cat shivered through me where her ankles had been, rubbing up against air. More funeral people came and the house got even smaller. I watched them take tea in the lack of space she'd lived in. I went to her room. It was full of two beds. I hovered above a bed. I came back through. I hovered above the sad. I hovered above the television. I hovered above the hoover.

They ate the salmon, the salad and the little sandwiches and they left, shaking hands with the man at the door, the father. They were relieved to be leaving. The blackness dispersed above the heads of most of them when they reached the garden gate and clicked it behind them. I went back inside the house to examine the left people. There were three. The woman was the saddest. She sat in a chair and the unspoken words which hung round her head said: although this is my home where I have lived for twenty-two years, and in it I am surrounded by family and familiar things, I do not rightly know any more where it is that I am in the world. The man made tea and cleared dishes. All afternoon while tea was being drunk or was skinning over he collected up cups on a tray and went through to the kitchen, filled a kettle and made more tea, brought cups back again full of it. In the kitchen he stood, opened a cupboard door, took nothing out of the cupboard, shut the door again. The still-alive child was a girl, another one. She had a fracture of anger starting under her yellow hairline, crossing her forehead and running right down the middle of her face, dividing her chin, her neck, her chest, all the way to her abdomen where it snarled itself into a black knot. This knot only just held the two halves of her together. She sat hugging her knees below the framed photograph of the gone girl. In it we were wearing a tie, shy, and holding a trophy in the shape of a swimming body.

There was some salmon left on the plate. I was wondering how it would taste. The man came through, took it away, scraped it into a plastic bag in the back yard. It was a waste. He could have kept it. They could have eaten it later or tomorrow and it would have tasted as good, better; I wanted him to know. I looked at him sadly, then shyly, then he saw me. He dropped the plastic bag. It rustled down on to the broken flagstones. His mouth opened. No sound came out (I could still hear perfectly then). I waved my swimming trophy at him. He paled. He smiled. He shook his head and looked through me, and then I was gone again and he threw the salmon away. A whole half a side of a fish, and the bones would have been easy to pick out, it was perfectly cooked. It had beautiful pinkness. This was last summer, my (suddenly) last. I could still see the full range of reds then.

So I practised the school photograph which was on top of the television. The face was innocence and tiredness, the age thirteen, a slight squint in the, the. The things she saw with. I honed to perfection the redness in them in another picture, one with other girls, and all the girls in the blur had red lights and mock boldness coming out of their faces and drinks in their hands. I checked to see I was performing the right girl. There she was, hiding at the back. I worked hard at the warmth of her look in the picture on the mantelpiece, the one with her arm round the shoulders of the woman now sitting so lostly in the chair. Her mother.

I could do the self in the oval on the headstone without even trying; it was easy, slight smile but serious; passport photograph for entry to other worlds. But my favourite to perform was the one with the left-behind sister in it too, a picture the sister kept hidden in her purse and only looked at after her parents were asleep or when she was in a room with a lock. Both of them sat on a couch, but the gone girl was caught in the middle of saying something, looking away from the camera. That one was my masterpiece, the angle of movement, the laughing look, the still more about to be said. That one took effort, to look so effortless.

From summer to autumn I did all that I can. I appeared to the father. I appeared to the mother. I appeared to the sister. The father pretended he couldn't see. The more he saw, the more he looked away. A wall crept inches higher from his shoulders round his head; every time I came he added a new layer of bricks to the top of it. By autumn the wall was way past the top of his head, swaying, badly bricklayed and dangerously unbalanced, nearly up to the ceiling in the living room where it knocked against the lampshade and sent light and shadow spinning every time he crossed the room.

I came only twice to the mother. It made her cry, made her miserable, jumpy and fearful. It was unpleasant. Both times ended in tears and sleepless weeks. It was kinder not to do it, and so I left her alone.

But the sister drained me with a terrible thirst. I couldn't appear enough for her. With the trophy, with the red lights coming out of my face, with the passport smile, with the laughing things unsaid. Every face I made drained and disappeared into the fracture that ran the length of her body. Summer passed, autumn came and she was still dark with thirst; if anything she was thirstier, she wanted more, and the colours were fading. When winter came I stopped. (It has been easier since then, I find, to appear to people who don't recognize what they see. I looked at the cracked face of the sad girl and knew. In the face of so much meaning it is easier to have no face.)

Above me the birds singing, further and further away. Each day a little further, more muffled, like wool in the ears. (Imagine wool. The rough-thready rub of it.) I sat an inch above the grave on cushy air. It was Saturday afternoon; I was bored with upsetting the family, bored with appearing to random people who didn't know who we were. The leaves were paling on the trees. The grass, neat and new, was greying for winter, and her underneath the sodden carpet, soil piled and turned for four luxurious feet above her. I looked at the passport in the oval, the face of the shape we had taken together. Down through the soil she slept. She couldn't come up. But I could go down. Down through loam and the laid eggs of many-legged creatures, and the termites, the burrowing feasty maggots, all waiting for it to break them open, the season after winter, I forget the word for it, the season when the flowers will push their heads regardless out again.

Down I went far further than stupefied bulbs till I passed through the lid of the wooden room, smooth and costly on the outside, chipboard-cheap at the centre. One last time I slipped into our old shape, hoisting her shoulders round me and pushing down into her legs and arms and through her splintery ribs, but the fitting was ill, she was broken and rotting, so I lay half-in, half-out of her under the ruched frills of the room's innards, cold I reckon, and useless pink in the dark.

The things she saw with had blackened. Her mouth was glued shut. Hello, she said through the glue. You again. What are you after?

How are you? I said. Sleep well?

(She heard me!) Fine till now, she said. Well? What? This had better be good.

I just want something, I whispered, to take to the surface. Just the one something. It's Saturday. Did you know? Your sister planted crocuses above your head last week, did you know?

Who? she said. What? Fuck off. Leave me alone. I'm dead, for God's sake.

I need to know something, I said. Can you remember the fall? Can you remember how long it took us? Can you remember what happened before it? Please.

Silence. (But I knew she could hear me.)

I won't leave, I said, until you tell me. I won't go till I get it.

Silence. So I waited. I lay there for days in the box room with her. I irritated her as a matter of course. I played with her stitches. I slipped in and out of her. I went in one ear and out the other. I sang songs from West End musicals (oh what a beautiful morning; all I want is a room somewhere / far away from the cold night air; cheerio but be back soon; sue me, sue me / shoot bullets through me / I love you), I sang them into the back of her skull till complaints rolling around from the neighbouring graves made me stop. Then I stuck her fingers up her plugged nose instead, tweaked her earlobes.

I missed three whole rise and falls of the sun (precious enough days to me if not her, lying now with her pockets full of soil and a dusting of soil over her so snug and safe in her shaft of days and nights that go on and on and on end-stopped by no base basement) before at last she said unblinkingly:

All right, all right. I'll tell you. If you promise to go away and leave me in peace.

Okay, I will, it's a deal, I said.

You swear? she said.

On your mother's life, I said.

Oh Christ. My mother. Ground rule number one. No reminding me, she said. And number two. Only the fall; no more, nothing else.

Okay, I said. That's all I want.

How much do you know? she said through teeth clamped tight. How far back do I have to go?

Well, I know about taking the dishes out of the little room, I said. I know about being careful. I remember curling into the room, tucking our legs in like someone not yet born, but I can't remember why. And I remember the fall, wooo-

hooooo you bet I do.

I kicked our legs against the thin-wood walls. I could feel she disapproved. With the sigh of one dead she said:

It wasn't a room. It was too small for a room. It was a dumb waiter, remember? –

(That's the name, the name for it; *that*'s it; dumb waiter dumb waiter dumb waiter.)

– and here's the story, since you're so desperate for one. Happy is what you realize you are a fraction of a second before it's too late.

Too late? Too late for what? I said.

No interrupting, she said. It's my story, this is it: are you listening? I fell in love. I fell pretty hard. It caught me out. It made me happy, then it made me miserable. What to do? I had expected all my life to fall for some boy, or some man or other, and I had been waiting and watching for him. Then one day my watch stopped. I thought maybe I'd got water in it and I took it to that watch shop across from the market. You know the one?

No, but I'll find it, I said.

Good, she said. The hands of my watch were stuck at ten to two, though that wasn't the right time. I took it off my wrist and put it on the counter and the girl behind the counter picked it up to examine it. She held it in her hands. Her hands were serious. I looked to see by her face what it was going to cost me, and when I did, when I saw her brow furrow as she thumbed and turned and shook my watch, when I saw the moment of concentration pass across her face as she held its face in her hands, I couldn't help it. I fell. She sells watches, all different kinds, and watch straps, and watch batteries. She sends people's watches away to have their insides cleaned out so they'll work again. She stands there surrounded by watches in cabinets, watches in cases, watches all up and down the walls, I had no idea there were so many different kinds of watch you could choose from, and all of them stopped, with their hands pointing to different, possible, times of the day. The only working watch in the shop that morning was on her arm, ticking into the warm underside of her wrist. She opened the back of my dead watch and checked the battery. Sekonda.

Is that her name? I asked.

I'm warning you, she said to me through her unopening mouth. I'm only going to tell you this once, remember? We made a deal. Sekonda was the word written on the watch, the name of the type of watch it was. It's the first word she said to me. Sekonda? like that, with a question mark after it. Mine's Sekonda too, she said. She turned her hand palm upward and showed me the face of her watch. It had Roman numerals. Then she said: it'll have to be sent away. It'll take about three weeks, maybe more. It'll cost around thirty-five pounds. That's average, but it could end up costing more, I've no way of knowing. You could buy a new watch for less. So do you want me to bother? Yes, I said; I couldn't think of any other word to say to her. It has to be fixed by specialists, she said. All the Sekonda watches get sent away. We can't do them here. Yes, I said, yes, and I took the receipt she was holding out to me and left the shop, the bell above the door clanging behind me.

I leaned on the wall outside the shop with the ringing bell in my ears. I held my sides with my arms. I didn't know what was the matter with me. I thought how I could go back into the shop and say, your watch is a lot nicer than mine, I'd like one with those Roman numerals, sell me one the same as yours. But I didn't move. I couldn't move. I stood outside the shop and listened to my heart ticking. I felt strange, and different.

Then I realized. I had fallen, and it was for the girl in the watch shop. I was happy. And I had a receipt.

(I stretched out on top of her in the room beneath the ground. There wasn't much space; it was lucky I am so insubstantial. The story had made me forget we were dead. But I looked and I saw the grim shut corners of her mouth folded down.)

So I balled the receipt up in my hand, she said. I kept my hand in my pocket and the receipt warm in my hand. For three whole hours that day I walked the streets as if I owned them, as if I owned the world.

Then I went swimming.

It was a warm day in May; I went to the outdoor pool. You remember the one, where they have the old-fashioned cubicles, wooden doors, the kind that swing open and closed like saloon doors from a western?

We used to love westerns, remember? I said.

No nostalgia, she said. Ground rules. What was I telling you? Yes. Go and look for the swimming pool too.

19

That day I swam like I'd been born to. I was happy, and the water skimmed me forward. I went back to my cubicle, slung my towel round my neck. I was rubbing my hair dry when I heard something going on, some commotion around the pool. I looked out. Two small boys were pointing at me. Some people were leaning over the side and gesturing down at me from the seats upstairs too. A girl, high up against the sky on the diving board, was watching, people were watching from below and above, all round the pool, even in the pool, leaning up against the edge and blowing water out of their noses; some were laughing. I felt cold run down my back.

But the cold I felt was just water from my hair; they weren't looking or pointing at me. Of course they weren't. They were looking at something near me, next to me. I stuck my head out further to see what it was, and this is what I saw.

A middle-aged woman three cubicles along was trying to close the doors on her cubicle. Only, the doors wouldn't shut. She wasn't that big a person but the cubicles on the women's side of the pool are small and her stomach jutted out, holding the doors open. She stepped out and tried going the other way in and the doors still wouldn't shut. They stayed open on the rump of her behind. So she backed out and tried going in sideways, but it was worse. It looked like she had been doing this to-ing and fro-ing for some time.

I got back down into the water and swam across to the other side. People made way for me, shifted so I could sit on the side of the pool with my legs in the water and see like them.

I saw like them. Now the woman had given up trying to close the doors and had begun to take her clothes off with the doors open, but there wasn't enough room in the cubicle for her to lift her arms or bend down so she stood outside it. She took off her shoes. She bent to peel down her tights and we could see the tops of her legs. Someone wolf-whistled. Everybody laughed. She put her arms up above her head to shrug her top off. Her face came out of her clothes, it was red and flustered. She was down to her underwear. We cheered at the swimming-guard who was running round the pool to stop her taking everything off. Another guard picked up her clothes off the tiles. One guard on either side of her, like a police escort for a shop-lifter or someone appearing in court, she was escorted out to cheering and clapping. She was barefoot, still wearing her skirt, just her underwear on top. We could see the skin pouched under her arms. A man called at her to cover herself up. I could hear female murmurs of agreement. No room for any water if she got into the pool, never mind room for the rest of us, the man next to me said; he was looking at my wet neck now, and I nodded and smiled because he was flirting with me, and slipped back into the water.

Afterwards everyone round the pool was high. I could hear them as I pulled my own clothes on over skin still so wet that the clothes caught and snagged on it. When I was on my way out several people said goodbye to me, like we were old friends, like we all knew each other well, had been through something together.

I was lying on top of my bed that night and my little sister was undressing to get into her own bed. She stared at me. What you looking at? she said. I had been looking. I had been gazing, without even realizing, at the shape of her body, at her stomach and the place where her pants covered her, and I had been thinking about what the girl in the watch shop's body would look like if it didn't have any clothes on it. It was the first time I had ever, ever thought such a thing, about anyone, and I felt shame in my gut and spreading all up and down my body. Nothing, I said. Well don't, fucking weirdo, my sister said and turned her back on me to pull her pyjama top on over her head before she unclipped her bra. When she turned round again she wouldn't look at me, but her face was red, like she was ashamed too. She got into her bed and snapped the light off and we were in the dark.

In the dark I decided to let myself think a little more about the girl. It was a lot easier in the dark. It didn't feel anywhere near as risky as it did to catch myself thinking about her with the light on. I thought about her until I heard my sister asleep, breathing like breathing was difficult for her.

I knew what my sister would think. I thought about what my parents would think; I could hear them through the wall, breathing. What our neighbours would think; they were breathing through the other wall. What Siobhan and Mary and Angela, and all the boys, all my friends from going to the pub, would think. What people who knew me would think. What people who hardly knew me or didn't know me at all would think. What the people at the outdoor pool, for example, if I were to take off all my clothes there in front of them right down to skin and thumping heart, would think.

My heart thumped.

I would go back with my receipt the next day and simply ask for my watch, and the girl would simply take the receipt, find my broken watch, give it back to me, and as she handed it to me over the counter she would simply look up, simply look at me, and see me.

The next day I went back to the watch shop. I stood outside it.

The day after that I went to the watch shop, stood outside it.

I did this for three weeks of working days, including Saturdays. Her day-off varied. Her lunch hour varied. It could be anywhere between half past eleven and four o'clock. Every day of the third week she had her lunch-hour at half past twelve, and every day of that week she opened the door, ringing its bell, waved back to someone still in the shop, let the door swing shut behind her, crossed the pavement, walked over the road, towards me, right to me, and right past me, inches from me. She was beautiful, and she looked straight through me as she passed me as if I simply wasn't there.

Falling for her had made me invisible.

On my eighteenth day of waiting, I let myself look for

one last time at the brown back of her jacket as she
passed. I went home. I shut myself in our bedroom. I
folded the receipt up as many times as it would fold, until
it pushed against itself in my hand, and I put it in the
music box on my dressing table. It was my mother's, from
the sixties, from when she was a girl. When you open it a
plastic ballerina unbends, flicks up and revolves on a
pedestal; she has one foot gummed on to it. She only has
one leg, meant to be two, stuck together. Her arms are set
in the shape of a circle. Her two hands are moulded
together above her head, her fingers are melted into
themselves. A tune plays as she goes round. Lara's Theme,
from Dr Zhivago. It sounds cheap. I forced the folded
receipt into the space under the pedestal at the end of
her leg. The music stopped when the lid went down and
the ballerina folded. I put the box back and got ready
to go out. I was in a hurry. It was my first night at a
new job.

On my first night a boy working on Room Service said
he'd show me the ropes. It was busy, it was the weekend.
On my second night we were up on the top floor. It was a
Monday. There were hardly any guests up there. I can't
remember his name. He told me the history of the hotel.
He had pockets full of replacement drinks for the
minibars. We were messing about, sitting on the beds in
empty rooms, watching their TVs with the sound down
and the subtitles on so nobody would know we were
there. It was quite early, about half past ten. He was
putting dishes into the dumb waiter. Under the metal

cover someone had left a steak and most of the chips. I ate
some of the chips. Don't do that, he said, I wouldn't do
that if I were you, you've not worked here long enough to
know where it's been. I said, I bet you a fiver I can fit
myself in there. I took the tray out. I nearly slopped gravy
on to the carpet, but I didn't, I put it down and I climbed
inside, I made myself fit it perfectly and I was just bending
my head round to say how much he owed me, when.

You know the rest, she said. You were there.

Our broken body at the foot of the shaft. I was there.
Wooooo-

hooooo, yes, what I felt, then. That reminded me. How
many seconds? I said.

Time's up, she said. That's your story. Go away.

But how long exactly? I said again. Can't you
remember how long it took us exactly?

No, she said.

What ropes did he show you? I said. Were the ropes
long or short? Did they make any difference to the speed
of the fall?

For fuck sake, she said. I've told you everything I know.

I was losing her. I tried another tack. You know that
swimming pool? I said. Did you ever dive off the top
board at that pool? Was it very high? Or the very top
boards of other pools? Because that's it, I reckon, the
same wooo-

hooooo only even more so.

Of course I did, she said. You know I did. I was good. I
could do double somersaults in the air. Look. This is

25

getting painful now. Go away. You said you would. I've told you. Don't you have a home to go to? Aren't you supposed to go to heaven, or hell, or somewhere?

Soon enough, I said (to God knows where).

Sooner the better, she said. I'm tired. Go away. Don't come back. We've no business with each other any more, and she closed like a lid. So I came back up. I left her there, in her sleep, unravelling each of the letters of our shared name and throwing away the little coloured threads that made it no one else's name in the world.

I want to ask her the name again for the things we see with. I want to ask her the name for heated-up bread.

I have already forgotten it again, the name for the lift for dishes. It has tired me out telling you her story, all you pavement-pressing see-hearing people passing so blandly back and fore in front of the front door of the hotel. I lose the words; like so many chips of granite tapped out of a stone to make the shape of a name, they litter the ground. I came up through the ground. A mouthful of ground would be something, dark and meaty, turfy and stony and pasting the tongue, graining under it and between the teeth like mustard. Or a handful of ground; grassy turf and the layer of earth crumbing down like good cake-mix if you rubbed it between fingers and a thumb, thickening like paint if you ran it through with a little spittle.

If I had spit, or fingers, or a thumb, a hand, a mouth.

You could put ground in your mouth, couldn't you? You, yes, you. You have a hand. You could hold the earth

in it. I came up through the earth and I couldn't keep
any of it. I flew over flyovers groaning with the weight of
their traffic. I saw rubbished grass round the edges of
stations; a dumped fridge; a burnt-out car; a piece of old
furniture rotten with rain. I saw the pool open beneath
me. It was drained and empty for the cold months. Dark
was coming. Old leaves blew in circles down at the
deep end.

On both sides the rows of doors rattled, fixed shut for
the winter. A sparrow waited till the leaves settled, and
hopped about at the bottom of the pool, cocked its head.
Nobody there. Nothing to eat.

I have a message for you, I told the sparrow and the
empty pool. Listen. Remember you must live.

The top board barely swayed beneath me, troubled by
thin air.

Where could I go? Back to the hotel. On my way I saw
a wall of faces shifting and falling like water. Here they
are: I saw a young woman struggling along a road; she
was carrying awkward things. I saw a man on the opened-
up roof of a house, white dust all over his hair and
bleaching his nose; he had a pencil behind his ear. I saw a
line of people; a man with his hands down the front of the
skirt of the woman standing with him in the line. He was
lifting her up by the groin; they both laughed, they had
the faces of happy drunkards. The other people in the line
stood between politeness and anger. I saw inside one
man's head; he was considering knives and blood.

I saw an old man with his hands raised after a much

younger man who was driving away in a car full of things.
The old man kept one hand in the air till well after the car
had gone, then he stood at his garden wall in the birdsong
and the nothing. I smelt pastry, faintly. In the cafeteria a
woman was sitting at a table reading a newspaper story
about a family who had gone on a boat trip and had all
but one been eaten by sharks. She read it out loud, severed
legs and bitten heads, to the woman behind the counter
who was laughing, horrified. Cigarette smoke curled and
caught as she laughed, staining her throat. I saw one car
in a remote car park in the early evening rain. It had an L
on the front and an L on the back, and inside it a boy and
a woman thudding against the seats. Ah, love. The full
weight of an other. The woman held a clipboard under
her arm, her other arm around the boy, who was boiling.
Steam rose from them both and slid itself across the
windows of the car.

I told them all.

I told all the people in the cinema queue. They were
waiting to see something. I told all the people in Boots the
Chemist. They were waiting for prescriptions. (Imagine a
glorious cold in the nose. Imagine a tweaking chirping
thrush in the groin. Imagine being a colour, and feeling
off it.) I went to the supermarket; the aisles were strain-
ing with foods. I told the check-out girls. They were
waiting for Saturday afternoon to be over. It was their
worst day.

Remember you must leave.

It was near dark. I found a shop with its windows full

of watches. A girl sat by herself, leaning an arm on the glass top of the counter. Below her were watches. Behind her were watches. She was staring at the front of her wrist where the moving hand on the face of her watch leapt and stopped, leapt and stopped, leapt and stopped.

I passed through her. I couldn't resist it. I felt nothing. I hope it was the right shop. I hope she was the right girl. She shivered at the shoulders and shook me off.

I put where my mouth had been to the side of her head. I said:

I have a message for you. Listen.

She flicked her head to sort her hair. She scratched at the back of her neck. She put her hand down on the counter again and watched her watch, the seconds, doing time.

Woooo-

hoooooo? Anything this time? No, nothing. I try again, and again. Nothing. Just sleep, coming. Time, nearly up.

It is my last night here. I circle the hotel and conjure stones, dust, soil. Some rooms are small, some are larger. The size dictates the cost.

I coast down corridors, invisible as air-conditioning. I waft about the restaurant from table to table, plate to nouvelle plate. I seep through the kitchen door; out the back five dustbins are stacked against a wall, each full of uneaten things.

I hang in reception like muzak. You will recognize me; I am a far-too-familiar tune. I slide up the shining banisters, up and up to the top floor, and through the door of one of the rooms and across the carpet and through the top window, and pirouette all the way down the front of the building (to the paving tiled with the name of the hotel, washed down every morning at half past six regardless of the weather or the dark or the light by the tired lady with the bucket and the mop, I shall not see her tomorrow, I shall miss). Woooo-

hoooooo I have a message for you, I tell the black sky above the hotel, and the windows lit at half past four down its sides and back and front, and its doors that go round breathing the people out and in.

Here's a woman being swallowed by the doors. She is well-dressed. On her back she carries nothing. Her life could be about to change. Here's another one inside, wearing the uniform of the hotel and working behind its desk. She is ill and she doesn't know it yet. Life, about change. Here's a girl, next to me, dressed in blankets, sitting along from the hotel doors right here, on the pavement. Her life, change.

Here's the story.

Remember you must live.

Remember you most love.

Remainder you mist leaf.

(I will miss mist. I will miss leaf. I will miss the, the. What's the word? Lost, I've, the word. The word for. You know. I don't mean a house. I don't mean a room. I mean the way of the   . Dead to the   . Out of this   . Word.

I am hanging falling breaking between this word and the next.

Time me, would you?

You. Yes, you. It's you I'm talking to.)

present historic

Else is outside. Small change is all she's made, mostly coppers, fives, tens. The occasional coin is still shining like straight out of a Marks and Spencer till, but most of them are dulled from all the handling and the cold. Nobody ever misses it, do they, a penny, that's fallen out of the hand or the pocket on to the street? There's one there, just to the side of Else's foot. Who needs one pence? Fucking nobody who is anybody. That's quite funny, the idea of fucking a nobody, just a space there where a body might be, and yourself flailing backwards and forwards against the thin air.

If she leans forward she'll be able to reach that one pence piece without having to get up.

She leans forward. It hurts to lean.

She stops trying. She'll pick it up when she moves on. She is

(Spr sm chn?)

sitting near a grating through which some warmth rises. This is a good place here outside the hotel, and it's hers, if she tucks into the wall alcove near the main door, good and decorous enough, far enough along from it to be left alone by the staff. She looks up. The sky is the ceiling. It closes in, dark early. On the highest ledge of the building opposite, the starlings have gathered and are settling and unsettling with flurries and jousts of their feet and beaks. Starlings' eggs: pale blue colour. They build nests with grass and feathers, sometimes with bits of litter, in trees or eaves or holes in stonework. They are real city birds. Their chests are punctured with stars. They swarm and turn in one grand gesture in the sky at dusk.

Dusk has already happened; the street between the buildings is lit by streetlights and the lights from the hotel front, the shop lights and the lights on passing cars. Else's neck hurts from looking up for so long. She drops her gaze down the side of the building. Yes. That girl is back, sitting on the steps of the World Of Carpets showroom. Yes, it's her. She's making it a habit. Everybody knows this is Else's patch. But that girl acts like she doesn't. She's got her hood up, but it's definitely her in there.

Else watches the girl. The girl watches something off to the side of Else. Else stops watching. Someone is passing, and is acting like she's noticed Else but decided to ignore her; most people don't see Else there at all, so it's a reasonable bet with one like this that if Else asks, she'll get.

(Cn y spr sm chn? Thnk y.)

Two ten pence pieces.

Put a ten pence piece in your mouth and bite down and if your teeth are soft they'll break on it. Which metal is harder, silver or copper? It is not real silver. It is an alloy. She will look it up in the encyclopedia in the library next time it rains, if the library is open. She has looked it up once already, but has forgotten. She is pretty sure it'll be the ten that's harder; it stands to reason. One time, she and Ade filled their mouths with as much as they could. He could get a lot more into his than she could; he had a bigger mouth, ha ha. It bulged his face out like a hamster; she could see the shapes of the edges of the coins pushing against his beard. It gives you a heavy head, money, if you fill your mouth with it.

It makes her laugh to think about. Laughing hurts. The money had been covered in saliva in their hands; he spat his into her hands, it came out like a kind of shining sick. You can have it, he said, you need it more than me. Jesus, they must have been drunk or out of it or something; they knew the dirt there is on money and they still put it all into their mouths. The taste was metal. After that when Ade had kissed her he tasted of metal too. He passed a ten pence piece into her mouth, in past her teeth and off his tongue, flat on to her tongue like a communion wafer, she held it on her tongue like it would melt, then opened her mouth and took it out. The date on it was 1992. God. They'd kissed all

(Spr sm chn?)

the different sizes of coin they had on them, back and fore, like a game, to see what each felt like.

Else tries to remember.

She can remember the taste of the kiss more clearly, even, than she can really remember Ade, what he looked like, his face. A whole time can reduce down to a single taste, a moment. A whole person down to the skelf of a self. Sometimes now she rubs a coin on her jumper and puts it in her mouth; silver tastes cleaner than copper. Copper tastes like meat gone off. The edging on a penny and a two is smooth; the edging on a five or a ten is cut with little grooves; though they're small they feel big to the tip of a tongue. The tongue-tip is sensitive. The weight of a pound is actually surprising. Else remembers being quite surprised. Nemo me impune lacessit. That's the promise of it. That's what the tip of the tongue can trace round the edge of heavy money.

The taste of it is always on her fingers, always lurking at the back of her throat. Or maybe the taste of money, or love, is just the same taste as the taste of catarrh.

Else looks up, across the road. That girl over there has her hood up today and people will be giving her less money because they can't tell if it's a boy or a girl she is. With her hood down she'd make a lot more. Though she's not doing badly. She's definitely doing better than Else. But with her hood down, well, she'd do a lot better. Else ought to go over there and tell her. She's got no idea. Ten past four she got here. She looks fourteen, maybe fifteen at the most; she's got school written all over her. She's got
       (Spr sm chn?)
good schoolgirl all over her face. Her hair is too bright and well, below that hood. She doesn't look hard up. Her clothes change. She has more than one coat. She looks like a runaway, but a brand-new, just-arrived-today one. So she gets money easily, of course she does, she looks like the stupefied baby animals looked on the front of the kind

of chocolate box that you used to be able to get years ago, if you compared them to a real cat or a dog. The only thing about her is that she looks miserable, she looks greyed. She's the colour of ice that's been smashed in over a puddle. Else feels quite sorry for her.

But it's not like that girl wants the money anyway. She doesn't even see them drop the money in front of her. Every time she's there it's the same; she makes a fortune she doesn't even seem to want in no fucking time at all. Else remembers what it was like to be that age and not to care. It makes them give you more, the people going past, so they'll matter to you. Some people even offer that girl notes. Else has seen this. They drop to their haunches in front of her and talk, shaking their heads seriously, nodding seriously, and the look on the girl's face is like someone's face would be if, if, Else can't think what. Yes, if that girl woke up and got out of her bed and went downstairs and out on to the street

(Spr sm chn? Thnks.)

and found that for some reason everybody else on the street, in the whole city, was speaking something she couldn't, like Norwegian, or Polish, or some language she didn't even know was a language.

People go past. They don't see Else, or decide not to. Else watches them. They hold mobile phones to their ears and it is as if they are holding the sides of their faces and heads in a new kind of agony. The ones with the new headset kind of mobile phone look like insane people, as if they're walking along talking to themselves in a world of their own. It makes Else laugh, and it's sore, to laugh. The sky is the ceiling, the buildings are the walls; she has the hotel wall behind her back now, holding her up. Inside her, another wall holding her upright, it goes from her abdomen to her throat and it's made of phlegm, and occasionally, when she can't not cough, when she has to cough, can't stop herself, the wall crumbles. She imagines it breaking like rotten cement. But it has its uses. It keeps her upright. It's holding her up just as much as the hotel wall is.

She imagines where her heart is, the muscles and the blood round her ribs and lungs. She imagines her lungs creaking and hissing, snarled up in blood and muscle like bad telephone lines, already outmoded anyway, and as if someone was trying to wire-up some place that just couldn't be wired up. Like if someone arrived carrying the telephone wires all waiting to be connected up, got out of his van and found himself standing outside some fucking great castle wall with thin slits in it instead of windows, and it was in the fifteenth century and there was no such thing as electricity.

(Spr sm chn?)

Think of him, Telephone Man, standing like something over-evolved out of Darwin, post-Neanderthal in his overalls with his wires in coils on his arms and his van full of great rolls of wire behind him and there he is scratching his head like a monkey because there's no metal grate in the ground he can lift to do the job, and a lady in a wimple peeking out at him through the slit like

40

he's a martian come in a spaceship because it's the
fifteenth century and there's no such things as vans. Think
of their faces. Laughing makes her cough. Coughing sends
– Christ, yes, she thinks as she coughs – a sheaf of
fifteenth-century arrows through her chest with all their
little flinty hooks and notchy metal edges, and that's just a
small cough, a choked-back cough, because a real cough,
she thinks daring herself, taking inch-large breaths,
recovering, would shake the foundations and send a
whole slab of fortress wall into the moat. A real cough,
she resets the muscles in her arms and shoulders, shakes
her head, is like the whole fucking National Trust ancient
fucking property breaking up into nothing but rubble.

Else is going to have to stop thinking. She's going to
have to stop using her

      (Spr sm. Chn.)

imagination. She daren't laugh again; she daren't cough
again. Who knows what she'll cough up? Something the
size of a baby fucking pig, by the feel of it, covered in
fucking pigbristle. Fuck. Cunting fucking. It coughs out
of her, satisfying and sore. Laughing makes her cough.
Breathing makes her cough. So presumably actual fucking
would make her actually haemorrhage. Moving makes
her cough; just her shoulders, her head. Else daren't
move, not just yet.

When she does decide to get up, this is what she'll do
She will go across the road to that girl, like she's done the
last twice, and pick up the money they've been dropping
at her feet. That's how they've decided to play it, her and

the girl, and that's how they will play it. First Else gets to her feet. Then she crosses the road. Then the girl sees her coming and runs away. Then Else picks up the money. It's fair. It's her right. Everyone knows the hotel is Else's. But she has to be careful how she plays it. She has to judge it right. If she gets up too soon she could chase the girl away too soon and miss out on potential money. If she doesn't get up the girl might up and go herself, and what if she took it all with her for once? what if she decided for once that she wanted it? Else steadies her breath. It'll be fine. In a while the home rush will start, a short while after that the home rush will be over; that girl could make who knows how much more in that time. Else will wait. She'll sit quietly and wait, because there could be ten or fifteen quid extra in it, say,

     (Spr sm chn?)

and that's fifteen quid more than Else can make, since she's making next to nothing today. You never make anything if you've got a fucking cough. They walk round you in a wide berth. Three pounds and forty-two pence she's made since night fell. So she could get quite fond of that girl. They've got quite a partnership going. Else could eat well tonight and maybe even buy some sleep too.

If the girl doesn't go first and take the money.

If Else can last out past rush hour and the girl is still there.

If nobody comes and moves them on.

Move along

People don't want to see it.

And I don't want to see it.

Okay?

That's the girl.

Thank you.

Some of the other things policemen and policewomen have said to Else over time:

Is that your stuff? Move it. Or we'll bin it. Move it. Move. (a man)

How old are you? You won't see another year at this rate. You know that, don't you? It's not just me saying that. It's statistics. They die every day, people like you. I'm not making it up. We see it, every day. You just keel over in the street. Don't you want to see thirty? (a woman)

You've got a home. Everybody's got somewhere. Go home now, there's a good girl. (a man)

Move along now, Else, we can't have this; you know we can't. (a woman)

Ever thought of working for a living? The rest of us have to. We can't all just loaf around like you. (a woman)

(whispered) Now I'm telling you straight and I'll only tell you once. You want a good raping, and you're for it. You let me see you in here again and you'll get it. I mean it. That's a promise, not a threat. You hear me? Hear me? Eh? (a man, at the station)

Can't you get it through your thick skull that decent people hate scum like you? You're scum of the earth. You spoil it for the rest of us. The scum of the fucking earth. (a woman, at the station)

43

Here you go, darling. Milk? Sugar? Give it a good stir, it's all powdered stuff at the bottom. (a man, at the station)

Did you have a look at the noticeboard up there, Elspeth? No? You're eligible for police counselling. It's on Thursdays, here, on the third floor. You're eligible. That means it's free, you don't have to pay if you're too poor. That's what we're here for, to help people. You only have to register. You only have to ask. (a woman, at the station)

Else remembers that word, from school. Poor. Then it was a word from history, from the times when there were such things as philanthropists (another word from history), which is what Robert Owen was, who built the workers in his factory a church and a school and a hospital, and didn't employ the very youngest of their children until they were a bit older than the age that other men who weren't philanthropists employed children at. New Lanark was the name of his mills, like his philanthropy made a new place in the world. The poor. What history worked to improve, to make things better for. But that was then. This is now. In one of the newspaper pages wrapped round one of her feet (her boots are too big) there is an article written by somebody suggesting that boxes for contributions of money, from people who have it for people who have to ask for it, could be set up in shops like Sainsbury's, so that money could still be given out by those who want to, but those who have it won't actually be

(Spr sm chn?)
asked for it by anybody. A deal like that (she dares a
laugh to herself and something in her chest ricochets, then
settles down) could put Else out of a job.

The penny by Else's foot, the one she will reach for in a
minute, is head-up, she can see, and it is quite a recent
coin, it has the paunchy head of the queen in her later
years. Else watches it. It's not going anywhere. She'll get it
in a minute.

She likes to wrap relevant things round her feet.
BRITAIN MASSIVELY MORE UNEQUAL THAN
20 YEARS AGO. ONE IN FIVE PEOPLE LIVES
BELOW BREADLINE. These subheadings are
cushioning her heel. Ha. She tore them out of the paper in
the library. This historic city she's sitting on the pavement
of, full of its medieval buildings and its modern
developments teetering on top of medieval sewers, is all
that's left of history now; somewhere for tourists to bring
their traveller's cheques to in the summer. Actual history
is gone. Else knows; she's clever, she always was. Today
she can remember how to spell philanthropist. But all the
same, today she can't remember which hand means which
on a clock, whether it's the short one that means the
minutes or the long one that does.

(Spr sm chn? Thnk y.)

Chn. Spr sm.

F y cn rd ths msg y cd bcm a scrtry n gt a gd jb.

First it's the thought of herself gttng a gd jb, with done
hair and skimpy smart clothes from the shops, legs the

45

fashionable colour of nylon and the right kind of shoe
strapped on, coming out of an office building like that one
over there above World Of Carpets. Then it's the thought
of the way she imagined it when she was a small girl with
her father on the Tube reading those gt a gd jb adverts
when they visited London, sharp-eyed girl with her hair
tied back and the neat clothes on that her mother had
made, way back then when reading the advert, knowing
what it meant, was one more proof of her cleverness in
getting it right, the shorthand for what was possible. It
makes her laugh. The laugh blurts out; she can't stop it.
The coughing does too, loud and sudden enough to spook
a passing dog who jerks on his lead and starts to bark,
and as the coughing and the barking racket out and an
arm drags the dog away, the coughing hurts, the stuck
splinter of herself as a girl hurts, the combination of the
coughing and the past gets her in its mouth like a dog gets
a rag, and shakes her.

   To stop herself shaking, to stop herself thinking of it,
she thinks of them instead, all the gd jb secretaries over
time, row after row of

         (Spr sm
         (pause to cough
         too long, person's gone)
         ch?)

shorthanders, 100-word-per-minuters. Think of them
neatly filleting the words, and their wastepaper baskets
overflowing with the thrown-away i's and o's and u's and
e's and a's. But they're all redundant now, she thinks, all

those scrtries. They're history. Ha. They've all been made redundant by crisp shiny new girls with dictaphone machines and computers which print up what you say at the same time as you're saying it. They're probably all on the street now, the scs, doing the same day's work Else does. She doesn't need vowels either. She knows all kinds of shorthand. She imagines the pavement littered with the letters that fall out of the half-words she uses (she doesn't need the whole words). She imagines explaining to the police, or to council road-sweepers, or to angry passers-by. I'll clear up after me, she tells them in her head. It's just letters. Anyway they're biodegradable. They rot like leaves do. They make good compost. Birds use them for lining nests, for keeping their eggs warm.

Starlings' eggs: pale blue. Robins' eggs: white marked with red. Thrushes' eggs: brown flecks or spots. Sparrows' eggs: grey and brown covered in splotches. Chaffinches' eggs: pink with brown tinges. Blackbirds' eggs: greeny kind of blue specked with brown. She knows the eggs of city birds; she has done since she was a child out in the back garden and looking in the hedge at the blackbird's nest, the three small green-blue eggs in the bed of grass and hedge-twigs. Don't touch them, her mother said. If you touch them the mother bird will know and she won't come back for them and they'll die. How will she know? Else asked. She just will, her mother said, I'm telling you, don't. Else was wearing yellow crimplene, it had a pink band at the neck, at the sleeve cuffs and at the hem. It was the month of May, nineteen seventy-nine, a very long time ago. The eggs were beautiful. She took out one of them and held it in her hand. It was light, it could easily break there in her hand. She could easily crack it; just moving a little would crack it. She put it back in the nest beside the other two. Nobody had seen.

The next day the mother bird still hadn't come back. Three days later the eggs were cold. The birds inside them would be mucus, their bones wouldn't have formed properly, would just be elbows of wing.

Stop crying, her mother said. It doesn't do any good for those poor baby birds. She handed Else a book, it had birds on the cover. The book made Else feel sore inside. She made herself learn facts out of it. By the summer of the following year, when rare heat shimmered at either end of the road and the nests hidden in all the trees and hedges were full of new fledglings and last year's eggs were nothing but a bad dream, Else (in a new blue cotton pinafore scooped at the neck, a daisy design sewn on to the pocket) knew these things off by heart: swifts' eggs were white and long, magpies' eggs were blue-ish speckled brown.

Nowadays this is Else's recurring dream: she enters a room whose walls are lined with wardrobes. She opens the door of the first one and inside on a shelf is her mother's sewing machine with the thick transparent Cellophane draped over it to keep the dust off. Round it, under it, above it, are drawers. Inside each of them is a complex filing system of folders. Inside each of these folders is a too-small garment. A dress, a cardigan, a waistcoat, slacks, a pinafore. Each piece of clothing has been made for Else. The folders fill the drawers and the drawers fill each of the wardrobes and the wardrobes crowd the room so that there is almost no space in it, and each piece of clothing is pressed flat in its folder, shrunk and airless as if vacuum-packed. Else is dizzy with them. She unpacks the first, and then the next, then one after another after another they pile up round and over her feet and even though she has opened hundreds of them there are still thousands more to unfold, all different, all handmade, all stitched with care and thousands more drawers of them waiting for her to open them. Puffed-sleeves. Tapers and waists. Pinking-shear edges. Zigzagged black braiding. Crimplene and cotton, nylon and wool, polyester and terylene and suede, and each of them is useless; too small, too fragile, too clean, too much; the wardrobes go on forever packed with unwearable love, and in her dream Else knows with a sheering hopelessness that she is asleep and that, untakeable as it all is, it will rip her apart at her seams one more time to have to wake up and leave any of it, one single piece of it with its empty arms, behind.

It is a nightmare.

It has got so that Else is afraid to sleep in case it comes, and afraid to sleep in case it doesn't come.

(Spr sm chn?)

She tries laughing. She coughs again. Nothing loosens. Her insides are blistered; she knows they are; they look like paint does when it's been too near heat. Her insides

49

are burnt-out like waste ground round a condemned building whose windows have been broken and their glass left lying about inside on the floors of its empty rooms. If someone went in there to try and get some sleep, say, she'd cut herself open on the glass. If she sat down to rest she'd sit on broken glass. When Else breathes, when she moves, it feels like broken glass.

She has shattered her insides, living the way she is. She knows she has. It isn't funny. It comes over her like misery. She has broken her insides, burnt them out, then heaped them over with ground as if to stop the burning. Beautie, Truth and Raritie. Grace in all simplicitie. Here enclosde in cinders lie. Enclosde, spelt backwards at the end. Nclsd. Shakespearian. Shksprn. The library here in this town is good. She thinks of the library instead. It is better than the one in Bristol. It stays open longer, generally, and the librarians rarely throw anybody out, even somebody getting some sleep. She has been reading metaphysical poets. Truth and Beautie buried be. Or: I am rebegot. Of Absence, Darknesse, Death; things which are not. Poetic darkness, Else thinks breathing carefully, has an extra e, as if a longer kind of darkness than the ordinary kind, and a capital D. Darknesse. Essence of dark. She has read a poem about a boy who acted plays in front of Queen Elizabeth the First, was good at playing very old men and died aged just thirteen. Else also likes William Butler Yeats. I went into the hazel wood. Because a fire was in my head. Go your ways, o go your ways. I choose another mark. Girls down on the seashore. Who understand the dark. She can't be bothered with novels any more. She has read enough novels to last her a lifetime. They take too long. They say too much. Not that much needs to be said. They trail stories after them, like if you tied old tin cans to your ankles and then tried to walk about.

Else panics. She has been dreaming and now the girl is gone. She can't see the girl. Is the girl still there? There are people on the opposite side of the road, she can't see past them. She can't see her.

It's all right. It's all right. The people go past and the girl is still there. She still hasn't moved. Her hood is still up.

She holds herself, that girl, as if she is all bruises. She's young enough for anything to have happened to her, and the way she stares at nothing it's pretty clear that something has. But on the whole she looks hardly tarnished; she looks shiny, out of place, like if someone left a spoon in the garden by mistake for a couple of nights, and there it is still lying in the grass exactly where they left it when they come to find it. She looks like she comes from somewhere with a garden, with garden furniture in it.

Else imagines the girl a garden and sits her on a sun-lounger. Tall flowers wave their heads. She is drinking a can of Coke. She looks disgruntled. Someone shouts something from a kitchen window. What? the girl shouts back, her head turned, her mouth open. What did you say?

No she doesn't. She doesn't shout anything. It's winter,

51

there's no garden, and she just sits there like that, a grey girl on the grey steps of the World Of Carpets showroom opposite in the darkness, watching the hotel.

She has the stupefied look of the lovelorn. That's what it (Spr sm chn?) is; yes. She is watching the hotel for someone going in, or someone coming out of it. Some man from up the road, some friend of her parents who's been having her regularly since she turned fourteen, on her jacket, spread under them on her mother's good corduroy front-room suite after school, or in the lunch hour, or while her mother is in the shower or out at the shops, and now his wife, or her mother, has found him out, or her father maybe, he's found him out, he's out to get him, he's going to punch his face in, they're searching for him, and she's come here to the hotel to warn him, she's sneaked out of her bedroom, out of the window and down the side of the house because the door was locked, they'd locked her in, she knows he said he'd stay in this hotel if he was ever

Or. She's waiting for someone to look out of one of the hotel windows and see her. Maybe some salesman who passes through town twice a month, who's just loosened his tie and opened the crotch buttons on his work-suit trousers, who's standing with his shirt-tail out, glancing at the night over the town, and – there, look – he sees her waiting so patiently for him, the, um, the (how would they have met?) the sly shy girl who was doing the teas and coffees at the sales conference two months ago, who teased him and whom he teased over the sugar packets,

whose virginity he thinks he pocketed between 10:45 a.m.
and 10:50 a.m. in the deserted Conference Room behind
the high stacks of seats, quick, because she had to be back
serving again on the hour and he had a demonstration to
give straight after the coffee break.

Ah, love. Else, laughing her guts out now, knows it
well. Members of the public, for instance, are always
asking her for it, as if it's part of her job to give it out to
them for their small change.

*Some of the things (concerning love) which members of
the public have said to Else over time*:

Fancy warming me up? (a man in a tailored suit)

Excuse me. I was just wondering if a twenty pound note
in fair exchange would be any use to you? (a man in
jogging clothes)

I am having a terrible day. I don't know what else to
do. I'm at the end of my tether. I don't know who else to
speak to. (a woman, crouching down and speaking near
Else's ear, putting her arms out to be held as she spoke.
Else thought about it afterwards. She had let the woman
sit like that with her arm through hers for nearly half an
hour; she had made herself available to her because it had
been a long time since anybody had given her the excuse
to think they were using her name like this. I don't know
what, Else, to do. I don't know who, Else, to speak to.)

Sure I can't tempt you? I'll give you a fiver? (the man in
the suit again)

How old are you? Would you like to come home with
me? (a woman in smart business clothes)

53

Want to come in the van, darling? I'll play you a tune. No? Sure? I've ninety-nines and everything. We can easy stick a Flake in it. (two men through the window of an ice cream van stopped at the traffic lights)

Are you okay? It's a cold one, today. How are you doing? See and keep warm now (a youngish woman, just being nice. But isn't it the same thing? Else wonders; doesn't it all come down to the same thing? Ninety-nines and just being nice, variations on the same tinkly tune?)

How much? (a boy, about thirteen. Else saw he was blushing round the back of his shaved hair. She charged him ten pounds, got the money up front and took him to the multi-storey car park. It was evening; Deck D was quiet and lit-up; there, in the smell of petrol and exhausts, on the concrete flooring between the back and front fenders of some small city cars: love. Occasionally now he passes her in the street. He's older; he hangs around with acned friends wearing tee-shirts with the names of American heavy metal bands on them. He looks hangdog, looks the other way. They never give her any hassle. He never gives her any money.)

Someone in a uniform has come out of the hotel's revolving door and is standing on the steps. A uniform generally means move along. Else stops, mid-cough. She becomes completely still. She has seen spiders and woodlice do the same thing. She is good at it. She will not be noticed.

When she next dares to look up the woman in the hotel uniform is crossing the road between the headlights of fast

cars. She sees her reach the other side, straightening
her tunic at the kerb before she goes on. She sees how
close she gets to the girl with the hood up before
the girl realizes and is on to her feet and away down
the alley along the side of the World Of Carpets
showroom speedier than any bird away from a sudden
cat.

Sht, Else says out loud. The girl's gone. She spits the
catarrh she's been holding on her tongue out beyond the
lining of her coat. She looks at where the girl was. Shit.
She starts to cough, and the coughing rips deep into her
till she can feel her insides split apart in a pink and riotous
cartoon zigzag like she has the ripped-bone mouth of a
shark opening from her throat down to

All right? Excuse me? Okay?

Else opens her eyes. The artificial stuff of the hotel
uniform is over her head. It reflects streetlight. She shifts.
She starts to gather up her things.

No, the woman in the uniform says, quick, putting her
hand out. No, it's all right, I'm not. Stay where you are,
I'm not.

Then the woman squats down next to Else.

Else can see her head and the side of her face, quite
close to Else's own eye; up close in the light from the hotel
the surface of the white of the woman's eye is pitted and
unhealthy. Else braces herself. But the woman is not
looking at Else at all; instead she is staring out across the
road into space. The embroidered badge on the lapel of
the uniform says, in browns and greens, *GLOBAL*

HOTELS. Stitched in white on the breast pocket there are small words. The top half of the circle says: *all over the world*. The bottom half says: *we think the world of you*. Else looks down hard at the ground. There are little bits of broken glass and grit in the crease where the hotel wall and the pavement meet. Some of the glass is green, some white. She can tell in the dark. Near it, a coin-shaped flattened wad of old chewing gum, part of the surface of the pavement. So many of the things on the street were close to people, intimate with them, even inside their mouths, before they ended up here.

The woman in the uniform is younger than she looks. She is sighing. She turns towards Else. Else looks away again. Four cigarette butts, two tipped, one lipsticked, one untipped, white and split, with shattered tobacco spilling out of it. One roll-up with its end pursed closed, a stained mouth itself.

They sit like this for what seems a long time to Else who counts, fourteen, fifteen, sixteen, the stitching on her blanket and the spaces between the crochet.

The woman snorts down her nose, like she is daring herself. She shakes her head.

Else looks hard at her own sleeve. Her hand. The top of her boot (her foot in it, asleep). Grime in the lines between the paving slabs. A cracked slab; something must have hit it hard; three cracks have spread from its centre. Her own spit, from inside her lungs, over there catching the light on the stone.

Listen, the woman says.

Though Else is still looking down and away she puts on her listening face, just in case. She is being careful. She doesn't yet know the uniform's game.

Do you want a room for the night? the woman says.

Ah. Else is not surprised, not really. Very little surprises her now anyway. She says nothing. She keeps looking down.

I work in the Global, the woman says. It's supposed to get even colder tonight. You've a bad enough cough; I can hear it all the way along in reception –

Else flinches.

– and it's supposed to get to minus six windchill tonight. We've a lot of rooms. Nobody in most of them. You'd be welcome to one of them.

Welcome, Else imagines the word, like it's written on a mat. Yeah, right. Now she will have to move pitch because people in the hotel can hear her coughing.

Of course, it would be for nothing, it would be for free, the woman in hotel clothes says as if she's suddenly angry at herself. You could get warm. You wouldn't have to pay or anything. No strings.

Of course, Else thinks. *Three things which come into Else's head in the few seconds after she hears the phrase No Strings:*

It is ten years back. She is in London. She has only been there for a couple of days and she has almost no money left. She is standing outside Camden tube station, and a man comes towards her. He looks all right. He looks clean, decent, like a Conservative party canvasser. He has money in his hand; it is new-born money straight out of a cash machine, not even creased. He says he will give her these three ten pound notes he is holding if she'll just come with him to his hotel room. She isn't to worry. She can trust him. No strings. He holds the money out. She can actually smell it, it's so clean. She takes it. The man waves down a taxi. She hasn't been in a taxi since she was a child. She sits on the long seat and the man sits opposite her on the folding kind. He looks distinguished. He looks a little like her father. He ignores her. They get out of the taxi at a station; King's Cross, she knows now; she didn't know then. Opposite the station there is a fast-food place. Outside it, written up above its doors on a sign, is a list of everything the place sells, spelt out, one letter after another. She points it out to the man while they wait to cross the road. *Look*, she says. *SALADSPIES*. It's funny. But the man isn't listening. He takes her by the shoulder as they cross the road and, still gripping her shoulder (she will have bruisemarks for about a week after), he pulls her up a sidestreet and buzzes an entryphone at a door in a wall. Someone somewhere inside presses something else which opens the door. He pushes her in. The stairs smell of disinfectant. Up two flights he opens another door with a key and shoves her inside the room. There is a man standing by the window. There is no furniture in the room, no carpet, nothing in it, not even a chair. *Get her to sit down*, the man at the window says. *I gave her thirty pounds*, the first man says. He glares at her. There's

only the floor to sit on. She quickly sits down. The man
shadowed with the window behind him is looking her
over. He comes across the room, nodding his head,
muttering under his breath. When he is right up next to
her he puts his hand inside his overcoat and takes
something out. It is a book. He opens it and holds his
hand up above her head, inches from her hair. He smells
of hair cream. For hours as she watches the light change,
from mid-morning to afternoon to early evening light,
the two men take turns to chant over her with their
book open above her head. They call for her to be saved
and to be forgiven. They talk about her as if she isn't
there. She gets up and leaves, when one takes a toilet
break and the other is in a kind of trance. The buzzer
door slams itself after her and she's back in the street.
People go past her. Nobody looks at her. She throws up
into a litter bin. Immediately after this she's hungry.
Back round the front on the main road, she orders a
kebab at the fast food place. She hands over one of the
ten pound notes and puts the change in her pocket,
where the other two notes are folded. *Your sign's funny,*
she tells the man who's cutting the meat off the revolving
stick. It is when she could still say whole words. *Your
sign. It says you sell salad spies. Salads. Pies. But it's
just one word on your sign, so it looks like salad spies.*
The man doesn't understand. He looks at her only
once, when he hands over her food. He has kebab fat
in his moustache. It must be a good place to work, if
he gets to eat there.

59

And: she is fourteen and just home from school. It is
four o'clock and Mr Whitelaw and she are having sex in
the front room. He was here when she got home. He has
been here, he told her, all afternoon, fitting her mother's
Venetian blinds all over the house. He is in his forties. He
looks like Patrick Duffy in *Dallas*, only a bit greyer. Her
mother is upstairs in the shower. She won't be able to
hear anything because of the boiler. *Christ*, Mr Whitelaw
is saying. His face is gleaming with sweat, his forehead
has furrows in it. They make her think of the run-rig
system of farming in Scottish History III. His eyes are
fixed on something just past her head. *The Woody
Woodpecker Show* is on the TV in the background. She
can hear the music and the drilling noise the bird makes
when it laughs. It strikes her that Mr Whitelaw could be
watching it over her shoulder. *Christ*, he says again, as if
he hates that programme. Then he says: *Elspeth. Let go.
Of my back. You're too tight. Don't hold on. Your nails
are. Jesus. Let go. You little. For fuck.* She is doing it
wrong. She is holding on too tight. She has to hold on
more loosely. For the life of her she can't think how to do
it. Then she remembers the puppet Snow White that
hangs on the back of her bedroom door. She imagines it
like it would be if she were to take it off the hook and lay
it out on the bed with its arms and legs loose on their
strings. She pretends her arms and legs are like that,
nothing to do with her, can only be made to work from
above. *That's. It*, Mr Whitelaw is saying. He scrapes her
backwards and forwards over the corduroy. She thinks of

the puppet's nose, made of a small tube of wood stuck on.
There is a Pinocchio puppet with an adjustable nose made
by the same people who make the Snow White. It makes
her want to laugh, when she thinks of the nose and she
thinks of Mr Whitelaw jutting out of his boiler suit when
she came in the door. She has to not laugh. She tries to
think of something different. I had strings, but now
they're gone, she thinks. There are no strings on me. She
thinks in the jerky tune from the film as her head hits the
arm of the couch. *Eh*, Mr Whitelaw is saying. *Good girl.
Elspeth. That's a. Good.*

Then, she and Ade are walking around Bristol in the
middle of the night. They are down near Brandon Hill
when they find an old man lying half in the road and half
on the pavement. He is pretty drunk. At first they can't
make out what he is saying, because of his accent. *My
legs*, he is saying. *I can't get up. My legs are not working.
Your legs are fine*, Ade tells him. *Come on, now.* They
stand him up on his legs. He smells of whisky and new
leather. They hold him up with their arms round his
shoulders. *I can't walk*, he says the whole time they walk
him home. *My legs have given out on me.* He tells them
he is seventy-two and tells them where he lives. *You're
blessed, so you are*, he says. *You got me my legs back.
Will you come in for a biscuit? I've a Family Box.* He lives
in a room in a block of other rooms. He switches the light
on inside the door. There is a toilet at one end with a
curtain that can be pulled round it. There is a sink, and
some cooking rings at the other end. There's a bed in the

middle of the room. The old man falls on to it. *My legs*, he says, *are not working right at all.* Ade's eyes are wide, he is staring. He points at the man's legs hanging off the bed. The man is wearing long cowboy boots with his trousers tucked in. They are shining; elaborately stitched; their leather is fawn-coloured and unmuddied. They have fringes at the knee and at the ankle. Within minutes the man is asleep and snoring. Ade pulls the boots carefully off the man's legs. They decide to stay the night; Ade thinks the man won't mind. There is a piece of cut carpet, quite big, by the side of the bed; she and Ade can fit most of themselves on it though Ade's feet are on the linoleum and hers would be too if she took them off Ade's shins. She flexes her toes. She runs her foot over Ade's legs; she feels how hairy they are, and how taut and good his muscles are, running the length of him. In the morning when she wakes up the first thing she will see is Ade's worn old boots there beside the amazing cowboy boots. Ade's boots are the shape of his feet. Laced through their holes, the green waxy string that keeps the boots on Ade's feet is knotted at its ends so it won't fray. That morning she will stretch the length of herself on the piece of crumby carpet and yawn, Ade breathing at her ear, and watch as the sun moves its white light across the two pairs of boots. She will remember it, that morning, that sun, those boots, as one of the times in her life when she was completely happy.

Now again. The woman in the hotel uniform is saying something but Else is dizzy and can't hear properly. She looks at the woman's shoes. They are recent and fashionable; they have thick soles of the kind of moulded plastic that looks industrial and prehistoric at the same time.

The woman gets up. She stops, stoops down again and picks up something. Here, she says to Else, holding out her hand.

In her thumb and forefinger is the one pence piece Else couldn't reach earlier.

Else nods, takes it.

Yours, the woman says. The one that got away. Nearly.

The woman straightens her back, and goes. She stands at the kerb again for a moment surveying the street, up then down.

Bye, she says over her shoulder to Else.

She walks back along the road and up the steps and disappears through the hotel doors. Their revolving glass flashes, dark then light then dark then light. Else holds the penny above the small pile of change by her knee. She drops it. It makes a single small clink when it hits the other coins.

Someone goes past, loaded with shopping.

(Sp sm chn?)

Nothing doing. Nobody else about. Else covers her money with the edge of her blanket. She pulls one foot out from under her, slow. Then the other, slow. She has to stop to cough. She tries to cough quietly, because they can hear her in the hotel. She gets to her feet by pushing against the hotel wall behind her. She is dizzy; she spits. It is always like this when she stands up after sitting. She gets her breath back and waits for the traffic to thin, then she sets out. The kerb; remember to step down. One step, then the next, then the next, then the next, then the next; halfway there. A car; wait. Another car. Now. One step then the next then the next, go on. The kerb; step up.

Else's heart jolts with delight. She coughs. She laughs. The girl has left the money and the money is still here.

She sinks down on to the step and counts it. Not bad, about thirty-two, thirty-three. Thirty-three quid in so short a time, good going. Ten times as much as Else has made. That girl could have made even more if she'd shown them her face. All the same. All the same. It has been a good day, Else thinks, one filled with luck, so far at least.

From over this side of the road you can't not see the hotel. It's like the street exists just for the hotel to be there in it. It sits squarely before her like a huge obedient dog. It is lit up from outside; up-lights spaced all along its front make it look rich, expensive and strange. Flagpoles jut out of it with no flags on them; flags are only in the summer for the tourists, Else supposes. With its awnings either side of its door, the building has a kind of face. The awnings are the eyelids, the word GLOBAL scarred across them both. As the building goes upwards its windows get smaller. Some of them are lit. None of them is open. Expensive drapes make each of them dramatic. She can see standard lamps standing between curtains. Round the ground floor at the front of the hotel are spike-topped railings painted white. Else remembers a girl at school who had a scar under her chin from falling on to some railings; a railing had gone right through her chin and mouth and tongue. She had had stitches.

The hotel's front door, massive in comparison to even the biggest of its windows, has the head of a child or angel or cupid carved above it in the keystone of its arch. The head has a feathered wing coming out of it, just one wing, its feathers spreading all the way round the sides of the face like an elaborate beard. A man once stood there carving that face, slicing lumps out of stone as if stone was cake or bread. The hotel building is quite old-looking. Else wonders how much the man was paid. A lot. Enough. Pennies, then. She wonders where the stone that was removed to make the head and its feathers, and the other curves of carving round the doors and the lower windows, went in the end.

She begins to pick up the left money. Winter-dark, winter-cold, winter-empty town. The streets have emptied. She won't make any more tonight.

It is starting to rain.

She could move to the pitch outside the video shop if there's nobody else already there.

The woman from the hotel said it would get colder. It's already cold enough for Else to be feeling it.

She could go to the winter-shelter. *The rules of the Winter-Shelter are as follows:*

   a.   This Winter Shelter is only for the use of people who would otherwise have to sleep rough.

b. No drugs or alcohol are permitted on the premises of the Winter-Shelter.

c. Customers of the Winter-Shelter are expected to behave appropriately when in the Shelter.

d. Customers are requested to behave with respect and consideration to our neighbours on their journeys to and from the Winter-Shelter each day.

e. The Winter-Shelter opens at 5 p.m. and closes at 9 p.m. Customers will be asked to vacate the Shelter by 9 a.m. of the following morning.

Else doesn't use the shelter when she can help it. It is a room full of deafening sleep, the coughing, snoring and shouting of dozens of sleeping or out of it people. The multi-storeys (there is a choice of three) are better, quieter, can be warm enough, depending, and you are less likely there to have to talk to anyone or have sex with anyone, depending which security man is on. There is nothing there but the sheen of empty cars and the oil-stained places where cars were and will be. The top decks are reliably quiet after eleven at night until seven in the morning. You can often find money there. It falls out of the pockets or the hands of the people looking for change for the ticket machine. There are lights that stay on all night. There are low walls that cut the wind out. There are good places to lean. There are cameras; it's safe. Nobody bothers you, depending.

She has a choice.

The flying head on the front of that hotel. What if you could grow feathers out of you like hair? That would be something, if your head could detach from your body and fly about by itself. Else wonders where her head would go, if she could take it off and hold it in her hands and then fling it up and set it flying, leaving her chest and her stomach and her legs and her waving-goodbye arms, her head soaring by itself up past the huddles of freezing starlings. The sky would open. The roof of it would come off. She would be so careful up there. She would avoid aeroplanes. She would perch on her neck-stem at the very tops of trees, she would land on the spike of the top flag-pole (careful not to let the spike pierce through her chin) and she would look down. She would survey the ground. The whole town would be below her.

Down there, over there, she sees her remains; her sleeping bag, her blanket, her day's takings. Where she sits each day is piled like a mistake, like rubbish, against the edge of the hotel.

She stops the imagining. It will make her go mad.

A taxi stops. Someone gets out and pays through the window, goes up the hotel steps and through the door.

She could stay in the hotel.

Tonight she could stay in a hotel.

That woman who offered her the room in the hotel; it is never as chancy, an offer from a woman, as it is from a man. That's common sense. Women aren't as strong, usually, and anyway they're less likely to give you a hard time, although they're just as likely to be lying. But she could check it all out. She could make a real noise if it wasn't okay. There's bound to be other people in a hotel.

67

A hotel has a staff who have to clean out rooms, or at least every few days they do. There would always be somebody about, eventually, if she was in any trouble.

No strings. Who knows what it means?

It could mean money.

It could mean something foul.

It could mean something good.

It could even be a disguise, a shorthand, for something that might make her happy.

Or it could mean something she doesn't know, can't know yet, something else. Something, Else. And there's no denying this has been a lucky day, so far. She leans backwards, stretches to touch the doorframe of the carpet showroom. Touch wood. This has been quite a good day. Whatever the game, it might be worth, in the end, her own room with a bed in it for the night.

She drops the girl's money in handfuls into the pocket of her coat, where it falls down into the lining.

She will cross the road and take the change she's folded under her blanket and put it in her pocket too. Then she will walk up the road like someone who is going to stay in a hotel. She will pass under the flying head. Now she can't tell any more whether she's just imagining it, as she pushes through the revolving door and into the blast of heat and the scent of meats and sauces that the air in a hotel is. Nobody stops her. She is walking on carpet that sinks like gracious mud, past chairs that are as big as she is. Nobody has stopped her yet. The reception desk comes up to her shoulders. The person behind it is on the telephone. She looks different, more frightening, in the light. She is speaking very loudly, and in an accent that has been clipped into a style. Something is clipping at her words as they come out of her mouth. Else imagines the clipping is being done by pinking-shear blades; narrow strands of irrelevant material stripped back, soft-tooth-edged, off the receptionist's words, dropped and wavering down to the floor and landing round her feet under the reception desk, like the swathes of speech that come out of the mouths of people in cartoons and holy pictures drawn and painted centuries ago.

The receptionist presses a button, holds the receiver away from herself and turns.

Can I help you? she says.

Then she says, Oh. Oh. Right. Can I, can I help you?

Else clears her throat and swallows.

A room? the woman says. For tonight?

Else nods.

The woman glances over her own shoulder; she looks younger when she does that, and nervous. Then she nods back, one nod.

For the one night, she says very loud. Certainly, madam. If you could just bear with me a moment.

She types something into a computer, then types something else. She presses a button. A bell rings somewhere down a corridor. Else gets ready to make a run for the door. Nothing happens. The woman stands up and reaches behind her for a key.

Else stifles a rising coughing. It will make her chest

burst, but she holds it in. The woman waits, her hands on the counter, till Else is ready. Else sees that she's wearing a badge with four letters on it. L. I. S. E. She wonders what it's short for.

Room 12, the woman says. Breakfast in our dining room is included in the price.

When the panic crosses Else's face the woman shakes her head, just slightly. She goes on reciting. Please don't hesitate to call down if there's anything we can do for you. Our bellboy will be glad to show you to your room. We hope you'll enjoy your stay with us here at the Global Hotel.

She is holding out a key. Else takes it. It is attached to a weight that is several times its size. The weight is bigger than Else's hand and wrist.

Fck sk, Else says.

A shaft of delight, like sunlight, crosses the receptionist's face.

First floor, she says smiling.

Else is inside. She is lying in the bath and looking at the taps.

She has looked at the little bottles of shampoo and shower stuff, so like the bright unthreatening colours of children's medicine that she has already opened one and tasted it on her tongue, as if it might have made her cough better. She has looked at the whiteness of the flannel and the cardboard band round it with the G of *Global* printed on it. Someone in a factory or workshop somewhere has wrapped up the soap in paper so that to use it you have to unwrap it like it's a gift. There are cotton wool buds and each one is individually wrapped. The fact that they are individually wrapped has made Else miserable. Now she can't stop looking at the taps.

These two taps have never been anything but dazzling. Every day someone has come in here and wiped them back to being brand new again. In every silver curve of them, in their long noses and the blunt snubs of their gleaming star-handles, she can see herself in a bath, distorted, pink and smudged, squeezed small and tight into the reflection. She has tried to find it funny. A pigmy. A circus freak. But she looms at herself, small and misshapen.

Water gathers at the underlip of one of the taps, wells into a drip and falls – it can't not – into the bathwater where it becomes more bathwater. Water runs down Else's face and down her breasts and does the same. Where it hits the water it becomes the water.

She huddles against the side of the bath and watches the taps and herself huddled in them.

What a coughing she'd had though, a really good one, one of the best; but not till the boy/man in the hotel uniform, who kept his eyes lowered all the way up the staircase and along the carpet of the corridor, had gone and the door was shut and locked behind her, nothing but her and the four walls and the bathroom, a whole other room behind its own door. Left alone in the rooms she'd roared and hacked like a lion. She'd bucked and snapped herself across the luxurious bed; it had hurt like fuck, like she imagines giving birth must hurt. Giving birth to a cough. Congratulations! Proud parent of snot and gob, twins, she hacks out a laugh. The noise she makes echoes in the bathroom and alarms her. The hot no-air in the bedroom had helped, tickling in her throat like a sick-feather. Then the satisfaction of coughing in a room that there's no one else in, really letting go into the silence of a place that's yours, a place where there's nobody to stare (or to not stare, which is, some days, worse). The pure rising satisfaction of dredging them up, your yellow old insides, and into your mouth and out, hawking them into the toilet water, hearing them spittoon in and watching them sink and flushing them out and away; that was good; that was really good; once the door was locked she had hammered at herself like hammering a rock, and broken it and spat it out, got as much of it up as she could into the clean mouth of the rich people's toilet and now, lying in the bath, with her clothes on the floor in a sweating pile and the sweat running down her, she is exhausted, still weak, bruised all up her muscles by it, but it was worth it, yes.

The hotel room is a collection of stuff, all matching. There is a fridge with drinks and chocolate in it; on the front of it Else read the notice: *Welcome to your Global Minibar. This Minibar is laser-set. Anything removed from the Minibar for more than twenty seconds will automatically register on your Room Account. A list of our Minibar Prices can be found in your Global*

Information Brochure. Global asks that you please do not store anything of your own in the Minibar, as this will trigger laser reaction. <u>Global Hotels. All Over The World</u>. The bed is good. It smells of a kind of cleanness that even shops full of things that haven't been used by anyone yet don't smell of. A small folded card on the pillow reads: *Please ring 0 for one of our staff to come and turn down your bed when you are ready to retire. <u>Global Hotels. We Think The World Of You</u>.* Else wondered when she read it if this is because there are so many covers; that the bed, being so thick with them all, needs two people if you want to pull them back. There is a carpet in the room, and cups with Gs on them; a kettle, a teapot and little packets of coffee and teas. There are several sorts of teas. Else has looked in a drawer. There was a hairdryer.

On the back of the door, *Room Tariff. Global Hotels. All Over The World.* A huge mirror. Else didn't look. The room has seven different lamps. Else has switched on only one. Hanging in the wardrobe, whiter than a ghost, a dressing gown made of towel. In the bottom of the wardrobe, a piece of stuff with a picture of a pair of shoes on it. A piece of paper. Else read it in the bath. *Valet Service, Name . . . Room . . . DRY CLEANING, suit 3 piece £10.50, Suit 2 piece £8.40 Jacket Trousers Overcoat £5.40 each garment Overcoat £10.80 Anorak/jerkin £5.80 Knitwear £3.90 Dress – day £5.00 evening £9.00 Skirt – plain £4.00 pleated £7.00 Silk blouse/shirt £6.00 Tie £3.00 waistcoat £4.90.* The piece of paper is on the floor of the bathroom next to her clothes, wet from her hands from her reading it in the bath. Else will have to dry it (she can do it with the hairdryer) before she puts it back in the wardrobe.

After the man/boy who had shown her where the room was had closed the door, Else had stood at the side of the room. After a few minutes she sat on the edge of the bed. It is a high bed; her feet were off the floor. She sat on it for a while reading about the things you can eat here tonight. Hamhock terrine pancetta salad taglionne of prawn w. garlic and parmesan venison sausages pommes purée crème brûlée grand marnier and seasonal fruits parfait. Then she had started to cough. Then, when she was finished coughing, she had tried to get the window to open, but it wouldn't, or she couldn't. Then she had decided to have a bath. She had taken off her boots, her socks, her jeans, her coat, her top jumper, her next jumper, her shirt, her undershirt and her vest, and carried them through to the bathroom where she could keep an eye on them.

Now she is in the hotel bath, looking at the taps.

She has been important before now. This is not the first time she has been it, and it is not just people in hotels who are it. There was the journalist last year, or the year before, in the spring, who brought a photographer with her who was photographing the things people on the street have in their pockets. Else emptied her pockets on to the pavement and the man photographed the things. The photograph was for a Sunday paper. The insides of Else's pocket have maybe been seen by thousands of people. The journalist had written down Else's name; the people who read the paper would have read that as well as seeing the things in the picture; the word of her name and the photograph of what was hers would have passed through the eyes and into the brains and maybe the memories of what could be millions of people.

She had forgotten about that.

She doesn't have any of those things any more, that she had in her pockets then.

They're just taps. They're just stupid fucking taps. All they can do is do what you make them do. They can't do anything else. Anything, Else. She reaches forward and turns the handle on the hot tap. She turns it as far as it will go. Water creeps up her sides. When it's too hot to stay in the water, she gets out, leaving it running, and when the water level comes to the edge of the bath she reaches to pull the plug out. The chain is too hot to touch. She wraps her hand in one of her socks, puts it in the water and yanks the chain up and her hand as fast as possible out of the sock. Almost as fast as water goes out of the bath, water is smashing back into it out of the tap. She sits on her clothes in the steaming bathroom.

She has decided against using the towels; they are too white, folded in their gross wedges on a glass shelf next to the toilet. In the bedroom she dries herself down on her jumper. She drapes the wet jumper over the radiator.

Someone in the next room or the room above is watching TV. Else can hear muted voices changing and muted music crashing into itself and making no sense.

75

There is rain on the window. She switches the light out. If that girl with the hood whose money she's got was sitting opposite now, she'd see Else with no clothes on standing in the window.

That'd maybe be worth thirty quid, Else thinks.

There's nobody at all outside World Of Carpets. There's almost nobody on the night street. A car passes; its engine is nothing but a swishing noise.

Else realizes the windows of the hotel are thicker than normal windows. They won't open.

She's too hot.

She watches another car pass. The lights of cars are always brighter on a wet road. The lit-up words of the World Of Carpets neon sign in the showroom's window throw colours on to the rainy pavement; orange, red, yellow; sleety rain mashes the colours. She wonders what it would sound like to stand behind the showroom glass, whether the rain can be heard there, whether the cars going past will be louder. She imagines sleeping in the showroom for the night. That would be something. It would be airy and cool in there. You could choose a different pattern of carpet to sleep on every night. You could choose it by the light that the neon sign gives out. You could roll out carpets that nobody has ever set foot on, be the first person in history ever to set your foot on them.

What about her blanket and her bag in the rain? Her stuff will get wet.

She should go down and get it.

She could go down and check whether the showroom has a back door, or a back window. She could go across there now. The rolls of carpet go right up to the ceiling. There's so much carpet in there.

When her jumper and sock are dry, she'll go. She'll get her things, and if there's no way into the showroom round the back she'll go to the multi-storey car park on Bank Street.

First, though, she could sit on the bed and count her money. She could pile the coins up, pennies separate from twos, twos separate from fives, fives separate from tens, tens separate from fifties, fifties separate from pounds in a neat sorted line, like an accountant out of a story or novel from a hundred years ago when the counting of pennies mattered so much that whole characters could be devoted to it.

Else sits on the bed naked and holding her coat, its lining heavy with small metal. She lies back. Her head is on firm cushions. There is sweat on her forehead, or bathwater, she can't tell. She closes her eyes. Inside her head she can still see the things the photographer took the picture of, the things from inside her pockets, arranged on the pavement. Beside them, her name. ELSPETH. She hadn't given them her second name.

Things from her pockets in the Sunday newspaper photograph:

The blue plastic clothespeg.

The pencil she found outside the bookies'.

That postcard, though it got folded and creased, that

she'd sent her mother and father when she went to
Venice, of a man in a gondola; an old-style postcard, the
colours all that fake kind of bright.

Some fusewire, rolled.

The packet of matches.

The teaspoon.

The comb.

The ten pence piece.

The taste of silver, metallic, rheumy.

The tap is still running, full on, in the bathroom. It
sounds like heavy rain. In a minute she will open her eyes,
get up and go. She pulls her coat up over her. Inside it
small change gathers weight, falls about. She tucks her
feet in under the coat. Although it's warm in the room
somehow it's cold too.

Her blood is pulsing. She can feel it. She can see it. She
can actually see her blood, moving inside her eyes, in the
collision of light and dark. Her irises behind her eyelids
bloom open and shut on the beat of its pulse like the
speeded-up heads of light-sensitive flowers or the sensitive
shutters of cameras.

future conditional

About you – continued.
If you need help filling in this form, or any part of it,
phone 0800 88 22 00.
Tell us about yourself.

Well. I am a nice person.

It was some time in the future. Lise was lying in bed.
That was practically all the story there was.

In a minute she would sit up. Then after she had
recovered from sitting up she would try to find the pencil
in the folds of the bedclothes, and then she would write
the words on the form.

After this she would cross out the word nice, and write
above it the word sick.

I am a sick person.

That's what she would do. She would do it. In a
minute. How many minutes were there in an hour? That's
something she used to know, to just know, like people
just know things. How many hours in a day, and weeks
in a year? That was the kind of thing children knew, the
kind of thing you were never supposed to forget in a
lifetime. But nowadays there were some days on which
she couldn't remember how many months there were

supposed to be in a year. Or which month it was right now.

It was summer, now, so it was one of the summer months, in the middle. She couldn't be sure which, or which it was of the months that had thirty days, and which had thirty-one, and which had thirty-two. Or even which day of the week it was today. Tomorrow she would (maybe) be able to.

Today, though, something she knew clearly was:
Mazola
Simply corn oil
Mazola
Lets the flavour through
You never taste the oil
You only taste the food
With Mazola.

The voice that was singing the Mazola song inside her head, the same woman's voice that had sung it years ago in the breaks between programmes, through the volume-holes punched in the side of the television, was friendly, reassuring. Mazola lets the flavour through. The pictures of the oil bottle and then the hands of a lady, delicate and ringed, letting chips fall on to kitchen paper and then shaking them off again, had demonstrated in a moment to millions how ungreasy the chips were, how little oil they left on the paper.

Lise breathed out. Then she breathed in.

Lise was lying in bed, in her room, in her flat, in a block of tenement flats six floors up, behind windows that looked out on to the walls of other tenements. Above and below her people were going on with lives. They scraped kitchen stools across floors, opened and shut front doors, turned televisions and radios off and on and shouted messages through the walls of rooms to loved ones or people they lived with. Outside, in the world, people still walked about and did things. For example, they went shopping. They could walk into a shop and not feel faint or dizzy or physically strange just because of the number of people buying things and the number of things available to them to buy all crammed inside the one roofed space with the noise of cash registers rattling out receipts for the bought things and the colours of all the products it was possible to buy swirling shelfily from aisle to aisle.

Shelfily. Was that a real word? She couldn't remember. She couldn't be sure. She blinked. Black came over her eyes with her eyelids, and lifted off again. Behind the skin and bone at the front of her head the Mazola song began again. Mazola, simply corn oil.

Lise was lying in bed. That was what she was doing. There was something she had to write down. She was waiting to remember it. Thoughts were slowly unearthing in her brain, like turf being turned up by someone she could make out only on the distant horizon, on the edge of a waiting field, a person made so small by distance and so slowed with age or weariness that he or she could hardly wield the spade.

Lise wasn't well.

Well: a word that was bottomless, that went down into

depths which well people estimated, for fun, by throwing
small coins then leaning with their heads over the mouth
of the hole and their hands cocked behind their ears
listening for their coin to hit the faraway water so they
could make a wish. What could well people find to wish
for, having everything already? Unwell: the opposite of
well. It ought to be a place where things levelled out, a
place of space, of no apparent narrative. Nothing could be
possible there. Nothing could happen there, for a while.

Instead Lise, lying unmoving in bed, knew; it was as if
she had been upended over the wall of a well like that one
in the last paragraph and had been falling in the same
monotonous nothing way for weeks, down into it like
Alice hazily pondering bats and cats, through nothing but
languid gravity, in a place where a second of time was
stretched so long and so thin that you could see veins in it;
and all these seconds, all this time, she (Lise) had seemed
to be hardly moving, though in reality the sides of the
tunnel were flying up past her at thousands, maybe
millions of miles an hour, the curved wall and its slime-
cold roughly surfaced bricks only inches from the skin of
her nose and chin and the knuckles of her hands and feet,
and her whole body tensed, ready, waiting, always about
to hit it, the surface of the water.

So there was a story after all, somewhere, insistent,
strung between this place and the last and the next, and
she was trying to remember it. But this morning all she
could remember so far went round and round behind the
hard bone of her forehead like the cheap advertising it

was. When it wasn't the Mazola song in there, sinuous with its oily promise, it was the altogether higher, purer voice of the woman who sang: Bring me apples, Bring me (something), Bring me hazelnuts, Bring me wheat, Bring me good things, To eat, Kellogg's Country Store.

This voice still sounded (inside her head all these years later) as if its owner had been brought up on healthy, very good things; it seemed to suggest that eating them every day had made her the successful and socially-upwardly-mobile singer of light classical repertoire that she was, and had got her the morally blameless job of singing on television about these good things precisely for the benefit of others.

Outside, the sun was shining. It was irrelevant.

There was something Lise had to write down, again. What was it?

I am a (   ) person.

She knew there was a pencil somewhere on the bed, or in the bed.

She didn't think she would be able to make it across the room to get the notepad off the window seat.

Deirdre would fetch it over when she came.

But Lise might need to write it down before Deirdre came. What if she remembered it and then had to write it down before Deirdre came in case she forgot it? She could write it on the telephone directory. It was right by the telephone. The telephone was right by the bed. It needed one moment of movement, that was all, to reach the telephone directory and then she could tear pages out of it and write on them. She could write on the front-inside cover, and after that on its first pages, on which there would be some spare space, and then in the spaces on the pages of listed numbers, or round their edges, in the margins; it was very unlikely she would run out of room. She was sure she didn't have that much to say. What she had to say about anything in the world would barely reach into the A's of the full lists of the names of the people who lived in the same area as her.

Tearing pages out, though, would be hard work. She could hold the telephone directory on her knee, but it looked hulking and heavy with the lives of the thousands of unknown people in it. And look, anyway, she had paper in her hand, folded, already waiting there in her hand. What was it, again?

About you – continued.

In a minute she would sit up, in a minute find the pencil.

Write down your symptoms, a doctor had told her. *Keep a diary of how it feels, what it feels like.*

Tell us about yourself. I am nice/sick.

Lise was lying in bed. A form had to be filled in. It was important. She was holding the form in her hand. It could have been in her hand for hours; she didn't remember anything like picking a form up or getting a form out of an envelope. She could have been asleep for days and awake for days, holding it. Who knew? She would ask Deirdre when she came. *Incapacity For Work Questionnaire Do not delay filling in and sending back this questionnaire or you could lose money*. How many days have I been holding this form in my hand? Lise wondered. Have I lost money?

Deirdre would know.

As soon as she could, Lise would begin it. I. As soon as she found the pencil. Am.

A nice person. I try to be one. I hold open the doors of shops I'm going out of or coming into for old people, or mothers with prams, or for anybody, for that matter, coming after or towards me, they don't have to be a mother or old. I flinch at television news showing dead bodies in different parts of the world, I feel for the relatives of the people killed, shown on the television grieving; I worry for people living in war zones. I worry for children whose parents or elders abuse them. I worry for people who are being tortured. I worry for beagles strapped into machines and made to smoke, and horses farmed for oestrogen whose foals are routinely slaughtered. I worry for vegetarians not having proper menus in restaurants, and for them having people be sarky to them because they're vegetarian, and I also worry for meat-eaters not being given their proper democratic rights, and smokers who are desperate for a cigarette and are stuck somewhere where they're not allowed to smoke. I worry for the lungs of smokers. I always help people with heavy things carry them up the steps of the bus. I am polite to people when we are standing in queues. I always let someone who has less to buy than I do go ahead of me at the checkout. When I'm driving, I am courteous. I keep to the speed limit, more or less, in built-up areas. I let people in other cars out of side-roads into the queue. I give way.

I am no great shakes. I am no saint. I am no world-changer. But I will put a cup or a glass over a spider on the floor, slide a postcard under with care so as not to catch its legs, and then open the front door and put it outside. Is that good? Or if there is overtime at the hotel and someone else needs it, I will give way. If someone asks me to work a shift for him or her, I will, of course I will, if I can.

Would've. Did. Was. Everything – cars, buses, work, shops, people, everything – other than this bed she was lying in was into a different tense now. Now: I am a sick person. I don't do anything. My skin hurts. My face hurts. My head hurts. My arms hurt. My shoulders and back and legs and feet hurt, at different times usually, though sometimes all at once. Pain travels round my body sticking little stakes into it like I am a new territory that has to be claimed. My hands act like they're made of stones. They weigh my arms down. When I walked to the doctor's – which didn't used to be very far, which is only a matter of hundreds of yards – though now a small room can be a desert, a vast and windwhipped plain from one domestic wall to the other – I found out what slow motion can mean. That was the last time my heart flew, and it flew inside me like a trapped bird, a blackbird caught in a living-room battering itself about above meaningless furniture.

I have not been out of the front door of the flat and down the stairs and out of the building since then.

How small this world has become. How huge that world is. I saw Paris on television. To see a city full of people walking, smoke rising, cars roaring, days happening, was terrifying.

I have since stopped watching television. My heart hurts. It hurts like a sore heart. Light hurts. Dark falls over me like a kind of apathy, and I am frightened that this apathy hurts too, that it is bruising me all over, and that one terrible morning I will wake up and find that I can feel it.

I sleep badly. I lie awake waiting till I sleep badly again.

I do not know when, or if, I will be able to do, well, anything, again.

Lise was lying in bed. She was wondering how to say all of this on the form.

Her doctor had nodded; *we can't actually find anything wrong with you*, she had said nodding. She was nice about it. There was nothing she could do. *You may have something as yet undiagnosable. Many people do. For instance your lymphocyte and monocyte count, here, are slightly raised. It could indicate that you've already fought off a small viral infection. It could also indicate nothing, it can indicate sheer normality.*

Lise was lying in bed. Deirdre would come at four. That was normality. All Lise could remember today was the songs of thrown-away rubbish; the songs of plastic bottles and cardboard cereal packets, things made and eaten long ago, long since rotted away or buried in landfill. Someone was to blame. It was Deirdre's fault, this, that all she could remember was rhyming trash. It was in Lise's blood like a germ; she had come down a bland line herself after all. Bland lines and forgettable bad rhyme were somewhere in her genetic structure, ha ha. She would tell Deirdre. That would make Deirdre laugh, maybe. At some point today, like all the days, it would be four o'clock. The moments would become minutes, then hours, and the hands of the clock would be at their jaunty angle and the door flying open and her mother would enter, all triumph and disaster. Perhaps this was medically relevant, something she ought to have told the doctor along with the headaches rheumatic and muscular pain backache migraine dental pain flu symptoms feverishness neuralgia nausea undiagnosable etc. Perhaps it was important. Behind me, under me, doctor, no listen, stretching down into the earth beneath me there are centuries' worth of ancestors who maybe suffered the same strain of bad art that's come down the line to me direct from my mother. Maybe you've heard of her? No?

Back then Lise the child had used to wonder where they all went, the thousands of faces of her mother on all the cardboard sleeves. Who had bought them and taken them home, what rooms they looked out on to. Where were they now? those smiles? that grooved-in voice? gone to LP-heaven? in second-hand stores stacked beside stolen stereos? down the backs of old-fashioned hi-fi systems in old-fashioned units next to old-fashioned three-piece suites in the houses of people's aging parents, alongside albums by Val Doonican and Lena Martell, Bobby Crush, Lena Zavaroni? At the height of her fame Deirdre had appeared weekly on a consumer television programme making up verses about news and current affairs. Her most popular poem, 'The Old Computer Card', had trembled on the edges of the top one hundred pop singles chart; a comic lament made by a computer card punched full of holes, about how new computers on the market had made computer cards obsolete. Deirdre had done a tour of regional theatres, she had signed many albums for smiling pensioners.

That was twenty years ago, when Lise was small. Now the pensioners were dead and her mother was greying, in her late fifties, and was occasionally on local radio where people made fun of her and imitated her unlocal accent. Over the years, the years had made her miserable. Deirdre, Queen of Sorrows.

But Lise being ill had made her happy. At four o'clock into the room through the door she would swing, come alive again, two-stepping to her own signature tune like the heroine of a middle-class sitcom into the sick daughter's room, a room that's not really a room but has been strewn by continuity people with all the tables and cabinets and things on the wall and books lying about that rooms are supposed to have, and its three walls open to an audience that's longing to laugh and clap, dying to laugh at any old rubbish, any bad line, any sick joke; an audience that's already been fleeced by a warm-up comedian telling them racist or mildly lewd stories. In would come Deirdre on cue to warm applause, all summer scarf and sympathy but happy, happy, happy, because at this particular time in her life (yes, one set of more or less consecutive moments in a lifetime of millions and millions of moments and exhausting possibilities) she was cheered, happier than she'd been in years, full of the new importance of her new major project.

What is happening to you, Deirdre told Lise in all seriousness, three weeks into her bedrest on the first of Deirdre's happier days as she knelt by the side of the bed and brought her face as close to Lise's as she could without her eyes losing their ability to focus, is visionary and poetic. It is like William Dunbar's poem, you remember? Man blown about like a willow tree is blown by the wind? *This false warld is bot transitory*? Remember? It is revelatory, to be sick like you are. It is a mystic state. Something comes of fevers in this world, girl of mine; prophets had fevers and visions; something will come of it. It's an ill wind, Lise, an ill wind, isn't it? Isn't it?

Girl of yours. Beyond Lise's tight-closed eyes Deirdre was smiling and eager on the carpet. She was almost quivering with eagerness. After a while of it, Lise had heard her get up, go through to wash her hands (she washed her hands a lot, in case it was catching). Her mother was humming in the bathroom, moving towels around. Here was real art at last. Three days later she announced her new epic poem, to be called 'Hotel World'.

Lise could, today, lying in bed, recall nothing more
than the fuzziest sense of what Deirdre had already read
out loud to her of 'Hotel World' – a metaphysical pun, of
which Deirdre was quite proud, on the Global Hotel
chain where Lise had worked – with rhymes like spiral for
post-viral, perm for germ, inspire us for virus. (Though if
you had been there and you had asked her yourself Lise
couldn't have remembered more than the odd word of it,
this is how verse four, for example, of 'Hotel World'
actually went:

> *You once worked on Reception*
> *In Control, my daughter dear.*
> *But now you find yourself checked in*
> *To your own Hotel Room, here.*
> *A room whose key's mysterious,*
> *Whose view is strait and serious,*
> *Whose purpose is imperious,*
> *Whose minibar is Fear.)*

Deirdre would sit on the end of the bed with her pen
held erect and wagging. Tell me a few little things, she
would say most days. Are you up to it? Darling? Up to it
today? It'll help you concentrate. Concentrate for Deirdre.
Lise. Lise? Tell me anything. Anything about the hotel,
for instance. Just everyday things would do. And when
she left at half past six she would still be saying as she
slipped out the door, and do remember Lise, if you can,
if you could, write them down for me as and when you
remember them, things that happened. Anything you

remember, anything. You never know what might be important.

The poem was only up to verse eight but it was going to be an epic; it allowed for a good long illness. But the point is, the point is, Deirdre would come. She was coming. Even in the timeless zone of the average day of an unwell person invisible to the rest of the fast-moving world there was Deirdre at four o'clock.

Lise was lying in bed and staring at the light-fitting. It was tiring just to lie in bed and stare upwards. Pains were jolting into Lise's head up through her neck. Inside her head they were kicking in the lining of her brain. They smelt of dung and animal. They trampled everything she knew. They were heavy as a herd of bison. They raised dust. Beyond the dust, the noise: *write down the things you can remember for me*, the poet-mother was saying. *Write down your symptoms*, the lady doctor was saying. *Fill me in*, the government form in her hand demanded. *Bring me apples, bring me something*, the Country Store lady, dainty and wholesome, was singing.

Bring me something. That was maddening, not to be able to remember what the missing something was in the Country Store recipe. Did it have two syllables or three? Lise couldn't remember. You never taste the oil. You only taste the food. There was nothing to make a rhyme of in the Mazola song but the word Mazola itself. Thank God. It was a relief. It was simple, corn oil.

How to fill in the rest of this form
Please use the boxes in the More Information sections

of each page to tell us in your own words how your illness
or disability affects you in doing day-to-day things. Tell
us about

> *pain, tiredness and breathlessness you feel while you*
> *are doing day-to-day things*
> *pain, tiredness and breathlessness you feel after you*
> *have done day-to-day things*

You do not need to attempt the activities set out in
the questionnaire. Tell us whether or not you could do
them, based on your experience of your illness or
disability.

*If you need extra space, please use the box on **page 18**.*

Lise was lying in bed. Was she lying? Was she faking,
lying, in bed? The form made her ask herself. It made her
nervous. *You probably aren't ill. Prove to us how ill you*
really are, it said. She moved as little as possible. She let
the pages fan open above her head until she found page
18. It was near the end of the form. The space on it was
about six inches by six inches. She would have to find
something to fill it with. She let her arm fall; it had been
in the air long enough for it to hurt.

She could fill it with something Deirdre would like to
be told when she came at four.

Deirdre would probably have liked, for example, to
know things like this. How the chambermaids Lise had
known at the hotel, or at least the more spirited of them,
had a practice of wiping down the toilet seats of excep-
tionally messy rooms with the face flannels of guests.
That they enjoyed trying on clothes that had been

unpacked by guests into the wardrobes and drawers of rooms when the guests had gone out of the hotel. That the going-through of guests' bags was mandatory. That a favourite thing to do was to switch on the battery-buttons of expensive cameras that had been left in rooms, so that the batteries in rich people's cameras would silently run down without them realizing.

Deirdre would also have been fascinated by the amount of spitting there was, blind random spitting regardless of who the guest or how big the tip, into room-service food and restaurant food in the kitchen of the average Global Hotel, and she would have been especially taken with the number of types of bacteria (including several usually found in urine) which could have been identified by a simple scientific examination of the surfaces of the peppermints left for guests signing in or out to help themselves to in the large misted-crystal bowl on the Reception desk behind which her daughter had worked for eighteen months after leaving college and before falling ill.

To be frank, Deirdre would have been delighted by or with any information at all, like being told about how heavy the sheets were for the maids to carry (sheets are remarkably heavy, and hotel staff are not generally allowed to use the guest lifts), or how new girls were taken by Mrs Bell into the room behind Reception and made to practise in their lunch hours with the ends of toilet rolls until they could fold the edges of the tissue to the right angle. (Not just to please me, Mrs Bell would say, rapping her pencil on the desk, but to show that care has been taken in preparing the Global's bathrooms; what's the watchword, girls? Customer Care. One new girl had been sacked, ostensibly for uncleanliness, but really for suggesting Mrs Bell's watchword was two words.)

Or, simply, unromantic unadorned information like how each member of staff received a piece of paper with a room chart on it in his or her pigeonhole every morning at six which told them which guests were staying and which weren't. This would have been of some use to Deirdre perhaps, or how the trick in Reception, when no bosses were around and it wasn't too busy, was to answer the phone saying *Good evening, Global Hotels, can I help you? Just one moment please, I'll put you through to Room Availability*, then to push button 9 (which relayed Mozart's Piano Concerto no. 23 through the receiver into the listener's ear), lay the phone on the desk, wait as long as you dared, push button 9 again and say into the same receiver, in another voice, as if you were another person, *Room Availability, Global Hotels, can I help you?*

Or how, when you work in a hotel, whatever it is you do – whether it's smiling at guests on the front desk or spitting in food in the kitchen, stripping beds of the smells of people or smoking against the rules out on the fire escapes, whatever – presses you hard, with your nose squashed and your face distorted and ugly, right up against the window of other people's wealth, for which employment you are, usually quite badly, paid.

All of these things, countless more things like this she

would have loved to hear, found useful to know, if only Lise had been able to remember them. Certainly making an effort to think about the hotel at all had brought something back into Lise's head today, for instance. But she couldn't quite get to it. It was something about baths, about a bath, something to do with a bathroom, and instead of it, in front of it in her head, was the voice of the TV-advert bottle of bubble bath singing along to the pictures of the bathtime children and their joyful mother. Your Matey's a bottle of fun. You puts me in the bath. I'm fun for everyone. I'm always good for a laugh. And while they splash in the tub. Your Matey gets them clean. So you don't have to scrub. No matter where they've been. There's one more thing to tell. Your Matey gets things right. So I cleans the bath as well. There ain't a mark in sight.

The singing bottle was shaped like a sailor. He danced around superimposed on everything Lise was trying to think. There were added s's on *put* and *clean*, to make the bottle's song sound more like real sailor's idiom. Remembering this made Lise, lying still and dizzy in bed, feel comforted. There were things after all, even minute details, that she still knew perfectly. She smiled, wan in the wan room. She wondered if the Matey song would be any use to Deirdre. Perhaps she should write it down for her. She would find the pencil. Singing bubble-bath bottle. That was something. She would write it on the form.

___Sitting in a chair___ *We need to know if you have any*

difficulties sitting comfortably in a chair. By sitting comfortably *we mean without having to move from the chair because the degree of discomfort makes it impossible to continue sitting.* By chair *we mean an upright chair with a back, but no arms.* **Please tick the first statement that applies to you.** <u>**Tick one box only**</u>.

I do not have a problem with sitting

I cannot sit comfortably at all

I cannot sit comfortably for more than 10 minutes, without having to move from the chair

I cannot sit comfortably for more than 30 minutes, without having to move from the chair

I cannot sit comfortably for more than one hour, without having to move from the chair

I cannot sit comfortably for more than two hours, without having to move from the chair

This form reads like a kind of poetry, she thought. Maybe Deirdre could use it, too. Maybe Deirdre wrote it. Maybe Deirdre is right. There is a kind of poetry, bad or good, in everything, everywhere we look.

Her eyes hurt. She closed them. Visionary. Poetic. Revelatory. Mystic. Yeah, Lise thought behind her closed eyes. It's true. Being ill is revelatory. It reveals to you exactly what well people think of ill people. They put flowers on the bed or on the table. They look at you with widening eyes. You look like death, they say, and then they laugh and add quickly, like it's all a joke, you look about as good as I feel. Then they look embarrassed (like they're letting the side down, ill people). Then they try to think up some imperfections of their own, and spend the hour telling you about them. Some of them expect to be made tea, or even lunch (you can't be *that* ill). Others are frightened to touch anything. They breathe, self-conscious, testing every breath. They look to the side of you as if you aren't there. They leave as soon as possible. For days after their visit they test themselves, listening for the press of glands and the slightest velvety creeping of skin, the tenderness of throat, the small knock-knock of symptoms. Who's there? Vi. Vi who? Vi Russ, we met at your friend's house, don't you know me? Don't you recognize me? Let me in. One day (maybe) Lise would be well enough again to go to someone's party and someone would ask her in that way that means who are you, *what do you do*, and Lise would answer with her new job description. I've been ill. I could not sit comfortably in a chair for more than thirty minutes. Now I cannot sit comfortably in a chair for more than two hours. It's hard work, but I'm getting better at it. And someone has to do it.

Lise was lying in bed. The room swung. The walls shifted then settled again. The idea of even imagining going to a party had frightened her. Every afternoon Deirdre put the telephone plug back into the socket on the wall. Every evening as her mother closed the front door behind her Lise yanked it out again. She could do it without getting up out of bed.

So imagine Lise's memory opening, now.

Imagine that when it did, it was as startling and

fractious to her as it would have been had the dead
telephone at the side of the bed suddenly started to ring.

Imagine her heart, leaping. Imagine her mind, sluiced
wide.

Lise, behind Reception, is at work. The clock on the
computer reads 6:51 p.m., but at the very moment she
glances at it the black 1 changes to a 2.

6:52 p.m.

She is pleased to have seen it happen. It feels meant.
Then she forgets about seeing it. Her neck is hurting.

The surveillance cameras at the front of the hotel are
out of action, including the one over Reception, so she
undoes her top button and pulls at the material round her
neck. She looks down at her Name Badge, LISE
backwards upside down. She undoes the pin on the back
of it, unhooks it from the uniform and throws it at the
waste bin up at the other end of Reception.

It misses. It falls down the back. She snorts.

She gets up, walks the length of the Reception desk,
leans down the back of the bin and picks the badge up
again. She jabs the tip of her finger with the end of the pin.

Ow, she says. Shit.

She slides the pin back through the fabric of her lapel,
clipping it shut. She sits back down on the chair. She
drums her fingers on the desk. She sees a tiny smear of
blood on the desk, and sucks her finger where the pin-
point went in. She wipes at the blood on the desk with the
edge of her jacket.

She is still high with what she's done.

She looks at the phone. She picks up the receiver, dials 9. She holds the receiver in the air for a moment. Then she puts it down again without dialling anything else.

She picks up a pen, puts the end of it in her mouth. She gets up. She presses the code on the door, letting herself out in front of Reception where the guests stand, takes the pen out of her mouth and leaves it on the desk.

There is no one in the lobby as she crosses it. The faux-coal fire is burning in an empty room.

She pushes the revolving door until she's at the steps on to the street, the surge of cold all round her. She stands under the Global Hotel sign and tries to see across the road.

She can't see anyone there. There's no one there.

She comes back into the surge of heat of the lobby. She straightens her uniform and walks across the room with brisk purpose. She lets herself back into Reception and sits down again. Her finger is still bleeding a little and round the place where the pin broke the surface the finger is reddened. She pushes the skin of her finger until the blood comes out in a perfect rounded bead of red. It is a surprisingly bright red. She puts her finger in her mouth.

Duncan is coming down the stairs, one at a time, slow. His head is down. He passes Reception.

Thanks, Duncan, Lise says as he does.

Duncan says nothing. He goes straight back into the LBR and shuts the door, so Lise talks to the shut door. I'll call you if we need you, she says. It's dead tonight.

She flinches at her own words. Shit, she says under her breath. But it's all right. Duncan won't have heard it through the combination of the shut door and the noise coming out of the speakers, flooding Reception, an instrumental version of 'Breaking Up Is Hard To Do'. Lise looks at the clock.

6:53 p.m.

Five hours to go.

She watches to see if she can catch the number on the clock changing itself again. But she looks away, just for the mere split of a second, and when she looks back it's already 6:56 p.m. without her having seen any of it happen or felt any of it pass.

It's already 6:56 p.m.: Time is notoriously deceptive. Everybody knows this (though it is one of the easier things to forget).

Five hours to go: Because time seems to move in more or less simple linear chronology, from one moment, second, minute, hour, day, week, etc. to the next, the shapes of lives in time tend to be translated into common linear sequence which itself translates into easily recognizable significance, or meaning. Lise is waiting for the next predictable point in the sequence: the time for her to go home. This week Lise is on evening shift. At Global Hotels, evening shift runs from 4 p.m. till midnight when the night staff takes over. In actuality here, when Lise thinks 'five hours to go', she still has five hours plus seven minutes till her shift officially ends, and usually there's also a loss of several minutes at staff changeover with the exchange of hellos and the putting on of coats; on evening shift Lise rarely leaves the hotel before 12:20 a.m.

Tonight, however, Lise won't leave the hotel building until 4 a.m.

Instrumental version of 'Breaking Up Is Hard To Do': Peter Burnett, undermanager of this branch of Global, chooses the music for the lobby. He ensures, by leaving three cds on low-volume repeat-play in the locked cupboard of his office, that nobody will replace his choice whenever he's out of the hotel building, including evenings. 'Breaking Up Is Hard To Do' was originally a summer 1962 UK hit for Neil Sedaka, and a hit again exactly ten years later in July of 1972 when television's The Partridge Family took it to number three in the UK charts. Some of the words of 'Breaking Up Is Hard To Do', remembered more or less correctly, are running concurrent with the background instrumental through Lise's head right now

    (don't take your love
        away from me
        don't you leave my heart in
        misery
        if you go
        then I'll be blue)

without her realizing they are, as she glances at the clock on the computer.

The speakers, flooding Reception: Figuratively speaking. More literally, in roughly an hour and twenty minutes from now the bath left running in Room 12 (one of the hotel's bigger, better and more expensive rooms) will finally overflow and flood not Reception but the bathroom, the room carpet and also part of the hall carpet outside the door of the room. The ensuing mess, found next day, will result in the sacking of Joyce Davies, chambermaid (28).

The tap left running will also cause three separate complaints from other guests in the hotel between 8 p.m. and 9:30 p.m. concerning the lack of hot water, complaints which Lise on Reception will apologize for profusely in the standard apology rhetoric of Global Hotels, log in the book and on the computer, and report to Maintenance.

It's dead tonight: Lise's stomach contracts; she has used the unsayable word, 'dead', to Duncan.

Lise talks to the shut door: This is apt. Talking to Duncan now, Lise thinks, is exactly like trying to talk to someone through a half-a-foot-thick shut door.

He goes straight back into the LBR: The LBR is staff-shorthand for the Left Behind Room; this is where all the things guests leave behind are stored until claimed or passed on to the police or taken home by staff members. It is less a room, more a large cupboard full of shelves and boxes of dated, labelled, alphabetically arranged things including: alarm clocks; batteries; books; all kinds of camera; cassettes and cds; items of clothing including gloves, hats, seventeen pairs of jeans; computer games; packs of condoms and a range of other kinds of contraception; many items of make-up; two mobile phones;

unidentifiable presents still wrapped in giftwrap; a prosthetic limb (lower leg); men's, women's and children's shoes (usually in pairs); small easily lost children's toys; various sizes of umbrella; cassette and cd walkmen, with and without earphones. The LBR smells of damp and plastic. It has no windows. It has a bare lightbulb. Duncan has been spending his shifts in the LBR, only coming out when he has to, for the last six months. He sits in the dark on a box labelled 16 Sept, Rm 16. The box is full of packed daffodil bulbs. Beneath him in the box in the dark some of the daffodils are beginning to sprout inside their packaging, and others are caving in inside their oniony wrapping, starting to rot.

Thanks, Duncan, Lise says: Most of the Global staff at this branch, at least those who were working here then, are protective of Duncan and his habits; they will happily rap on the LBR door to let him know whenever Bell or Burnett are around so he won't get caught. Everybody who works there knows Duncan saw what happened, he heard it, he was on the top floor with Sara Wilby when she did it. Newer staff members tell each other in low voices that he should leave or be asked to leave. They discuss the rumour that he refused compensatory redundancy. They discuss what it must have been like, to be there. They discuss suicide. They discuss love. They implicate Duncan. When Duncan goes past, the hush of no one speaking trails in front of and behind him, eerie, like embarrassment. Lise likes to make him do a little work, small things, whenever she's on with him. She thinks it will be good for him. Lise used to think she might sleep with Duncan one day, when she first worked here. He was funny, he was sociable, he took risks, he was quite handsome. Now it makes her uneasy to be on the same rota as him. She is kind to him. (She is invisible to him.) Secretly she thinks he needs therapy.

She puts her finger in her mouth: The body's logical urge towards natural antiseptic.

The finger is reddened: The local inflammatory response of the body's coagulation system.

She walks across the room with brisk purpose: In six month's time, Lise will be incapable of walking across a room with brisk purpose. She will be almost incapable of walking across a room. Even the thought of a word like *brisk*, the ghost of the word passing across her mind, will have the capacity to cause her anxiety. One night in her sleep (which for ten months of her near-future life will be a restless, pierced state) she will dream that she is on the back of a black and white pig and that the pig is galloping, almost flying, at a dangerous speed over a landscape, fluid beneath her, that looks like Wales or the Scottish borders. When she wakes up from this dream she will be exhausted and panicked. Her heart will feel burnt. Her leg muscles will hurt where she gripped the pig in her sleep. This will be one of the low points of her early invalidity.

She straightens her uniform: Lise has momentarily forgotten that the surveillance cameras are off and that the straightness or otherwise of her uniform will not tonight be reported to or recorded by any authority.

No one there: Not literally true. There are some people outside on the street, passers-by in cars and on foot. This *no one* particularly refers to the fact that there is nobody on the pavement opposite, where Lise is expecting or hoping to see the adolescent girl who has been sitting on the pavement or sheltering in the shopfront opposite the Global.

She can't see anyone there: *Anyone* here refers to the same *no one*, above. Lise is sure she recognizes this girl from the funeral of the dead chambermaid, Sara Wilby. Sara Wilby (19) worked briefly at the Global before falling to her death the previous May in a freak accident, the tragedy of which was reported on both local and national news (25/26.5.99) and caused first, the three-day closure of the hotel and second, escalated demand for rooms on the hotel's reopening, demand which remained high well into late summer with locals and members of the general public all keen to see the location of the death.

Global Hotels made it compulsory for members of staff from this branch to attend Sara Wilby's funeral. After the funeral a joke went round the hotel staff combining the Doris Day song 'Que Sera Sera' and the dead girl's name. Lise can't remember the wording of it now but she remembers it was a relief to pass it between themselves, illicitly like a spliff, as they all did at work in the weeks after the funeral in the hotel kitchens, in the hotel storerooms, and walking back and fore in front of the door of the boarded-up basement. Jokes the punchlines of which were, for example, *Well and truly shafted* or *Sara*

Wilby in a lift or *Because she offered to go down on him* had been Chinese-whispered up and down the stairwells of the hotel right into the autumn months, though by now they have, so to speak, died down.

Lise had spent time on one of the same rotas as the dead girl. The dead girl had had dark hair, but it was a Saturday, busy, and there was always new staff coming and going, there were always new chambermaids, chambermaids have high turnover. (High turnover: a phrase full of punchline potential.) Sara Wilby's family had stood at the church door. All the people who worked at Global filed past, bosses first then undermanagers then administrative staff then Reception then Security then Maintenance then Kitchen then Cleaning, and shook hands with them. A couple of weeks ago Lise realized that that's where she knew the girl from, the girl who had been sitting outside across the road. Lise had seen her at the church door as they all went past in their hotel uniforms. Lise thinks she may have shaken that girl's hand.

Tonight Lise went out of the hotel to speak to her. She was going to ask (but the girl ran off) if there was anything she could do, if there was anything the girl wanted, money or a coffee or food or anything, if she'd like to come in and warm up in the hotel, if Lise could do anything for her or help her in any way. Can I do anything for you? Can I help you in any way? She had had the words ready.

Lise knows that she (Lise) must have known Sara Wilby. She was on that same rota for the first of the two nights Sara Wilby worked at the Global. She definitely must have spent some of that evening's time with Sara Wilby, she must have spoken to her, they must have exchanged at least looks if not many words. But though she's tried, she can't really remember anything about it. She can't even remember what Sara Wilby looked like that night, two nights before she died. It is much easier to picture her from the photographs in the papers and on TV than to try to remember. The photographs in the papers and on TV seem to have wiped Lise's memory of the real Sara Wilby even cleaner.

It's for this reason, for exactly this blank in the memory where there's almost no face, almost no body, nothing but the near-empty outline of a person not known – and also because she is a nice person herself, and just in case there's anything she can do – that Lise is keeping an eye out for, has just checked outside one more time for, that girl who has been spending her evenings sitting on the steps of the carpet showroom opposite the front of the hotel.

The lobby: All branches – British and international – of Global Hotels have identical lobby design by Swiss interior designer, Henri Goldblatt. To list all regulated details here would take up too much space; Goldblatt's original blueprint featuring several specific furniture and fabric manufacturers is over ten pages long. For front-of-lobby flowers, on page 6 for instance, Goldblatt specifies stargazer lilies.

Global International plc Board and Shareholders

believes that site duplication within still-individual archi-
tectural structures reinforces attitudes of psychological
security, nostalgia, and preserves the climate of repeated-
return in worldwide Global clientele.

The lobby of the branch at which Lise works smells of
good carpet, distant restaurant food and stargazer lilies.
In bed ill in six months' time, Lise will be unable to recall
the precise scent of the Global lobby. In two years' time,
on holiday in Canada and desperate to get out of a sudden
spring snowstorm, she will shelter in the Ottawa Global
and as she enters its lobby will unexpectedly remember
small sensory details of her time spent working for
Global, details she would never (she will think to herself
afterwards, surprised) have imagined she even knew, and
which remind her of a time in her old gone life before she
was ill and before she got better, a time which she has
almost completely forgotten she had.

Takes the pen out of her mouth: In the course of the
evening Lise's saliva on the end of the pen slowly evapor-
ates into the conditioned air of the lobby. It will be an
hour and forty-five minutes before the pen is completely
dry.

Where the guests stand: As Lise passes in front of
Reception she briefly imagines, as she always does, what
it would look like to see herself working behind the desk.
She imagines, only for a moment, that she is the well-
dressed young woman who came in earlier, someone
whose stays in hotels like this one are paid for with the
credit card of the national Sunday broadsheet for which

she works; someone whose year of birth is the same as Lise's yet whose clothes come from shops where even the air hanging over the clothes is exclusive; clothes blessed by the smell of money, unbuyable in this town or this part of the country even now in new postmodern Britain, in any case unimaginable on any real body with any real walking, working or sweating to do. She imagines that, standing there signing the forms, she sees herself (Lise) on the other side of the desk; a hick stranger, a good but unimportant worker. A neat no one – it is important, behind Reception, to wear hair tied back and to wear 'subtle' make-up. There Lise is, there she can see it, her subtly made-up face above her Name Badge, sleek and smiling, emptied of self, very good at what she does.

This imagined moment makes Lise, in reaction, feel stronger, better, angrier, more determined from the base of her spine to her shoulders. It fills her head with foul language. Also, although the hotel is quiet tonight with many good rooms free, Lise has given this woman one of the less pleasant, smaller, less viewy rooms on the top floor. In a calculated shift of social power a little later tonight Lise will enjoy punching the number of the room (34) into the Reception phone and letting it ring, just once, at the other end, so she can imagine the woman full of dashed expectation, hand hovering above the receiver.

Lise has also thought she might, much later tonight and provided she can catch the night staff off guard, take the security key off its hook on the wall and go up to the top floor, let herself silently into the rich woman's room and stand over the rich woman in her bed as she sleeps unawares. This is an act Lise has fantasized about before tonight, though not yet carried out, being generally too nice a person. But tonight, for Lise, anything is possible (or at least, many more things than are usually possible; see below, *Still high with what she's done*). Also, at the moment Lise's sensitivity about money is heightened. Last week when she put her cash card into a cash machine outside her bank the machine kept the card. When Lise went into the bank the next morning to ask for it back the assistant behind the counter refused to give it to her. The assistant, who was much younger than Lise and who regarded her with blunt suspicion, said the card was property of the Bank and that Lise, about whose overdraft the Bank was extremely concerned, was now to be issued with a new card which would allow her to take out only a fraction of the money paid into her account by her salary cheque. The account is called the Solo Account. It is usually given, Lise has discovered, to people aged fifteen. The assistant asked for Lise's chequebook so she could *make a note of its details*. When Lise passed it through the hole under the partition, the assistant ripped the book in two and put it in an envelope and the envelope in a drawer which she locked. *We cannot allow you to write cheques any more, Miss O'Brien*, the assistant said. *This chequebook is property of the Bank.*

Later tonight, however, Lise will leave the hotel carrying a wastepaper basket full of small change.

Tomorrow morning when she wakes up slumped over her kitchen table she will find the wastepaper basket by the washing machine and will count the change; it will come to nearly twenty-five pounds. She will be pleased. She will remember paying for a hotel breakfast out of this money, and buying some croissants and a pint of milk for her own breakfast from the all-night bakery on her way home. The croissants will be in the bag still under her work clothes. She will split them open, put them under the grill and run downstairs to the shop for butter. She will eat them heavily buttered for lunch and feel rich, unexpectedly lucky. All tomorrow evening her work clothes, which she hasn't had time to wash, will smell of the faded scent of croissants.

The code on the door: 3243257. Unless these numbers are pressed in the correct order on the code-box on the door, the door will not unlock. This is normal safety procedure.

In six months Lise will be unable to remember this code. She will never need to remember it again.

Holds the receiver in the air: Lise, excited, cannot decide whom to call to tell about her act of letting a homeless person have a room in the hotel for the night. The friends who would understand what she's done all work for the hotel too, and could mindlessly or mindfully betray her to authorities. Other friends who don't work for Global wouldn't understand its full rebellious significance and the combination of temerity and courage it has taken. Lise is torn for a moment with the idea of calling her mother,

Deirdre O'Brien, who would understand the ramifications of the act but to whom Lise, at this mid-twenties stage of her life where her judgement and resentment of her mother are more weighty than her understanding of their complex relationship, has no real wish to speak, wanting instead to have adventures whose power is in their being withheld from, rather than gifted to, her too-fast aging, formerly publicly embarrassing, mother.

9: The number which must be dialled first for an outside line from Global Hotels.

***Still high with what she's done*:** This evening Lise, by inviting a homeless person to reside in the hotel for the night free of charge, has probably broken all Global Quality Policy. In doing this, she has made herself feel better.

Lise has seen the homeless woman quite often outside the hotel in the past. The homeless woman sits in the sun, wind, sometimes rain; she resembles a buddhist meditating, her palms up and open. Lise has thought it must be a rough life but a good life, a freed-up life. She thinks the shift in homeless people over the past few years is an interesting one; old drunk men and middle-aged mad women before; now, younger and younger. Lise, unable to make out the age of the homeless woman in front of her at Reception, was also unprepared for the strong smell she brought into the lobby with her, though she is still pleased to be doing someone the world of good for one night. In a spontaneous act of generosity, she will list Room 12 on the computer for tomorrow's Room Service

115

Full Breakfasts. (Though a moment later she will panic about this and then erase her listing because it bears her initials; the computer is running under her shift password. It is, however, more or less safe to have involved Duncan; Duncan is taciturn, and Bell and Burnett are both still a little afraid of him after the accident and are unlikely to question him about it, should anyone find out. She is hoping, as he takes the homeless woman up the stairs and as she waits for him to come down again, that the scam might excite him out of the LBR tonight and maybe even into some conversation, like in the old days.)

Drums her fingers on the desk: In a rhythm approximating the opening lines of the first verse of Neil Sedaka's 1962 UK chart hit, 'Breaking Up Is Hard To Do'. See above, *Instrumental version of 'Breaking' etc*.

The fabric of her lapel: Global Hotel uniforms are 78 per cent polyester, 22 per cent rexe. They induce perspiration.

Waste bin: Lined with plastic, this waste bin contains only an emptied Advil blister-pack (Lise's) and a plastic container labelled St Michael Pasta and Spinach Salad With Tomato and Basil Chicken, now empty except for the used white plastic fork (originally belonging to Mr Brian Morgan, guest in Room 29, who asked Lynda Alexander, day shift Reception, to dispose of this when he checked in at 2 p.m.).

Smear of blood: Type A Positive.

Name Badge: Name Badges are part of Global Quality Policy. The Quality Policy Training pack (UK1999) states: *Quality is doing things the way they should be done, first time, every time. The way we measure quality is to find out just how much money we spend sorting things out. We spend over one day in every four sorting out things we've got wrong. We have a lot of very complex processes, which people at different levels contribute to. The Quality Programme is about getting people to do better all the worthwhile things they ought to be doing anyway. If we can do things better and cheaper, we can handle growth more easily, have happier customers, happier staff and happier managers.*

Nobody on the staff at this branch of Global is quite sure what any of this means, other than that it's something to do with the difference between good and bad and the need for better. The main change brought about by the installation of Global Quality Policy has been the wearing of first-name Badges by lower staff, and full-name Badges by line managers and managers.

Surveillance cameras at the front of the hotel: The wiring of the surveillance cameras through to the Security Office at the rear of the hotel building was carried out (under slack supervision) by an apprentice electrician. The front unit power cuts out every time a chambermaid catches the wire with the side of her trolley wheeled at a certain angle along the back corridor.

The system not functioning properly has given Lise the opportunity to offer Room 12 to a homeless person in the knowledge that nobody from Security will have been able to record her actions.

Her neck is hurting: Lise's glands are raised in her neck, under her arms and in her groin. At present she is aware only of a slight discomfort under her ears and chin which she imagines is coming from too tight a neckline on her uniform.

The clock on the computer: The clock is at present running 12.33 seconds ahead of GMT.

The computer can provide information on hotel guests, staff, international tariffs and more general Global matters. It lists in its staff files (to which only certain members of staff have access) the payment details and home addresses of all members of Global staff, including those of Joyce Davies, chambermaid, who lives at 27 Vale Rise, Wordsworth Estate, and will first thing tomorrow morning be fired from this branch of Global Hotels by Mrs Bell, who believes (having been assured first by both Lynda Alexander and Lise O'Brien, day and evening shift Reception, that Room 12 has been unoccupied) that Davies has neglected to attend to Room 12 over a period of two days and is therefore directly or indirectly to blame, in the absence of any responsible hotel guest, for damage caused to the Hotel by a bath left to overflow. The cost of damages, £373.90 for replacement and drying, will be removed from Davies's final paycheck.

Lise, behind Reception, is at work: There she is, Lise, behind Reception, at work.

The lobby is empty.

In a moment, she will glance at the clock on the

computer and see the moment when the number changes
on it, from a 1 to a 2. She will be pleased to see it happen.
It will feel meant.

That is then. This was now.

Lise was lying in bed. She was falling. There wasn't any
story like the one you've just read, or at least, if there was,
she hadn't remembered it. All of the above had been un-
remembered; it was sunk somewhere, half in, half out of
sand at the bottom of a sea. Weeds wavered over it. Small
stragglers from floating shoals of fish darted in and out of
it open-mouthed, breathing water.

And even if she had remembered it, what use would
the memory be now anyway? If dropped into water, for
instance, like soluble aspirin, would it dissolve through-
out to form a solution? Could it even partially numb the
aches of all the kinds of quotidian pain that aspirins can?
Light and fevered, Lise's world spun; in its spinning the
names of all its places were loosened and jettisoned off
the sides of it, leaving seas and countries nothing but
blanks, outlines waiting to be rediscovered and renamed,
their longitudes and latitudes stretched and limp as done
elastic. It spun so relentlessly and fast that its bridges
spontaneously combusted, its buildings burned, its skies
were implacable. Its birds on their jabby ashen sticks sang
dusk and dawn and daytime apocalyptic choruses. You
only taste the oil, the blackbird sang on the charred
garden fence. You puts me in the bath, the wood-pigeons
whooed deep in the flaming sycamore leaves. Bring me

good things to eat, the swallows squealed as they fell through smoke and rose and fell again.

Somewhere – it was promised – there would be cleanness, a scrubbed-fresh feeling; there would be cornfields, trees, air, pure healthy foodstuffs; there would be goodness, simplicity, clarity; there would be balm for sore limbs.

Lise was asleep.

Four o'clock.

Lise's mother put her key in the lock, turned it, pushed the front door and came in. She did all this with conscious tentativeness. Her hand held itself back so that it almost shook.

She came through to Lise's room quietly. She got her face ready to say hello. Lise was asleep. The hello face wasn't necessary. Her mother kept it in place, in case Lise should wake up.

It was seven steps from one room to the other in Lise's flat. Her mother crept through to the kitchen, held her breath, pulling the door over so Lise wouldn't hear the rattling of the bags. She breathed out, opened the cupboard. She unpacked into it the things in tins and boxes; tuna, beans, mackerel, muesli. She put the tomatoes and the new potatoes and the salad and the salad dressing and the gravadlax and the small organic fruit yoghurts in individual pots into the fridge. Soon she would buy Lise a new fridge, if Lise would let her. She put the fruit in a breakfast bowl and, after she'd wiped the breadboard down, the bread on the breadboard. She put the soup carton by the cooker for later, ready for when Lise would wake up.

Lise's mother opened the door; it creaked again. But Lise hadn't woken. Quiet she crossed the carpet to plug the telephone lead into the wall-socket; quiet she sat down on the carpet, leaned against the wall and watched her daughter, the fearless child Lise, the imperturbable twelve-year-old, unreadable sixteen-year-old, unruffleable girl, impenetrable adult, Lise. Lise lay in the bed. She was pale, crumpled, frowning, dark, sleeping. She breathed unevenly.

Everything in Lise's mother's body hurt, because it hurt just to be near her daughter. Lines were edging themselves into her face as she looked at her. She looked at the bed instead. There were papers on it. Without disturbing Lise, she picked the booklet up off the bedcover. About you – continued. Standing. We need to know if you have any difficulties standing. By standing we mean standing by yourself without the help of another person or without holding on to something. Using your hands. Please tick the first statement that applies to you. I cannot turn the pages of a book. I cannot pick up a two pence coin with one hand but I can with the other. Seeing. Speaking. Hearing. I cannot hear well enough to understand someone talking in a normal voice in a quiet room Controlling your bladder. Tick one box only. Other information – continued. Please use this space to tell us any thing else you think we might need to know.

There was something written in pencil in the box on this last page. Lise's mother held it up to the window light so she could read it. It was hard to make out. It was two words. It seemed to be the word *bath* and then the word *singeing*, or the word *singing*.

She put the form down on the bed. She watched Lise breathe. She watched the nothing happening in the room. She would keep watch until Lise woke up.

She leaned forward to put the back of her hand against her daughter's forehead, to test her temperature. Gently she lifted the hair off Lise's face, tucked it behind her daughter's ear, away from her eyes. She sat back again, up against the wall of the room.

Ah, love.

perfect

With one finger of one hand Penny typed words. With the other hand she pressed numbers on the hotel TV remote control.

Classic, she typed. Ideal.

A country and western star on the TV screen told the camera how much God loved Nashville. He loves it, she said. It's a place in America, a part of America, that's especially loved by God.

Fawless, Penny typed. She deleted the F and replaced it with an l. Then she put the F back on the front again.

Classic Ideal Flawless, the computer screen said.

She flicked channels. This hotel TV had a decrypted porn channel, maybe left over from the last guest. Two girls with waggling apparatuses strapped to them were taking turns at each other while a man in leather underpants encouraged them by slapping their bottoms and grunting. Penny watched. Her mouth fell slowly open. She screwed up her eyes. As if it knew she was watching it, as if it had been waiting for her to, the channel crypted over.

Damn, Penny said.

FFFFFFFFFFFFFFFFFFFFFFFFFFFFFFFFFFFFFFFFFFFF
FFFFFFFFFFFFFFFFFFFFFFFFFFFFFFFFFFFFFFFFFFFF
FFFFFFFFFFFFFFFFFFFFFFFFFFFFFFFFFFFFFFFFFFFF

FFFFFFFFFFFFFFFFFFFFFFlawless, the computer screen said.

Penny laughed. She deleted the extra Fs. Words appeared on the TV screen telling Penny to type in some numbers on the remote control to buy the channel back. Penny got up off the bed and looked at the piece of card that hotels put round their remote control sets, but she couldn't find the pay-per-view digits written on it. She looked under the television, which was silent now, its screen blank. She looked all round the desk and in the drawers. She thumbed through the information booklets about the local restaurants and the local theatre. She climbed back on to the bed, sat crosslegged again in front of the laptop and tried punching random numbers into the remote. 3554. 8971. 1234. 4321. She leaned over and picked up the phone and dialled 1 for Reception. But there was no answer, and when she turned to put the receiver back in its cradle she pressed the channel-forward button on the remote with one of her knees by mistake.

A sharp-suited man in a TV studio was telling something to a man in a sweater, who was standing up in an audience of what looked like old and out-of-work people.

But she's there, right there, the man in the suit said. I'm telling you, there, yes, there, he said into the microphone. She's slightly to the left of you, at your shoulder. Who is she? Is she your mother?

Penny lit a cigarette. She blew smoke out; it disappeared above her head.

126

My mother's not dead, the other man said. This is my mother here. He gestured to someone sitting beside him in the audience and the camera found her face; it was lined and befuddled, lit up by the sudden camera light so that it looked visited, divine.

Immaculate, Penny thought. Immaculate, she typed.

The audience on the TV was laughing. The man in the suit had suddenly put his hands up over his ears. Whoever she is, she's really yelling now, he said. Who is she? She's yelling loud enough to wake the living.

The audience laughed again.

I have an aunt that's dead, the man in the sweater said. It might be her.

Do you know what she's yelling now? She's yelling, *I'm* not dead, the suited man said. He put on a high voice. *I'm* not dead, he said. Don't call *me* dead! *I'm* not dead!

That's her, that's my Aunt Alice, the man in the sweater said. That's definitely her. That's uncanny. That's just what she was like.

Penny pressed the off button; the signal crossed the room invisible; the TV shut down. She sucked the end of the cigarette, blew smoke out in a sigh. All the people who have ever died, still here; ranging and loping over the earth and all its countries, bobbing about in steerage crowds wider than the seas themselves, or standing in bulky lines jammed all over the world like nose-to-tail cars on three-lane motorways into London and packing the cities, towns, shops, offices, rooms, even maybe this hotel room, standing behind their invisible wall and beating it with their fists and all of them soundlessly shouting it, *We're* not dead! Don't call *us* dead!

Uch, Penny heard herself say, and tried to shake it out of her head, but she couldn't stop the thought which expanded all by itself to include dinosaurs that had been reduced to the imprints of their own vertebrae in rocks and slate, and woolly mammoths as big as houses matted and frozen deep in Russian ice deserts, and lions and tigers shot and skinned, and the beheaded stags she'd seen in drawing rooms and restaurants, the dead pheasants that had hung in her father's outhouses rotting for better taste. Then the horses and dogs and cats she had known (and her heart contracted, she couldn't help it, at the thought of their gone warm muzzles, the thought of their hoofs and clawy paws, the unique furred sides of them and the lit liquid of their eyes, the horses bumping around in the grounds of the house, the dogs jumping and rolling and yelping hello, the cats with their tails in the air, vanishing ahead of her along the polished corridors and up and down the main and the back stairs). Not just these, she told herself, to push the thought on and away from what it was making her feel about animals dead and gone years ago. Zoo animals too, she thought blankly, species after species from aardvark all the way to zebra. And what if all the chickens and their eggs, and cows and their calves, and the different kinds of fish, and the pigs and sheep and lambs, all the hundreds of creatures that she herself – just her, nobody else – had eaten over this half-lifetime she'd had, were waiting there too, and the ghostly chirruping above them of all the birds which had ever flown across her range of vision, momentary visitors to it. All the mice she had ever seen garotted in traps and all the rats and foxes poisoned, dead on their sides with their tongues hung out. The one-day-long butterflies, and the moths she'd watched charring themselves on light-bulbs, and bluebottles swatted, yellow and burst. All the small fruitflies which had grazed her life on their uneven flightpaths, the tiny hardbacked beetles which lived in the roof beams and which she sometimes found in her bed and crushed between her finger and thumb, even the airborne germs that lived and died and passed in their invisible billions through just her system alone. All of them, all of them, all of them, battering the wall she couldn't see with invisible fists and paws and hoofs and antennae and amoebic thready stem-things, yawling and hooing in all their mute languages, barking and squawking it, snorting and mewing it, mooing and braying and squealing and squeaking and humming and hissing it, Hey, you! *We're* not dead! Don't call *us* dead!

What an infernal noise, Penny thought, blinking. What a terrible endless noise. It's just as well we aren't actually able to hear it. Remember you must die. Remember you must diet. Penny laughed out loud, got her pen out and made a note of it. But with the TV off and the sound of her own laugh fading she could hear too much silence now, and round behind the silence the anonymous shiftings of people in this dreary building who had no idea who she was or that she was even there, and the anonymous streetlit scufflings of this dreary one-theatre late-evening town beyond the hotel in the high view from her window.

She made herself listen instead to the workings of her finger at the keys on the keyboard in front of her on the bed as she picked out the right letters for the right words.

Superior, she heard herself type.

Transcendent.

She thought for a moment, holding her chin.

Leaving nothing to be desired, she typed under the other words. Oh, that's good, she heard herself say out loud. It leaves nothing to be desired. It left nothing to be desired. If you're on the hunt for somewhere which leaves nothing to be desired. If you're looking for the classic place, the ideal place, the flawless place, the immaculate, no. Superior place. Transcendent, no.

She deleted transcendent and immaculate.

Superior place leaving nothing to be desired, she said to the empty room round her. The room responded by closing in on her. Its walls loomed down, its ceiling lowered like the threat of bad sky.

The bathwater had been lukewarm. Penny had called down to complain. In any case the water that came out of the taps had looked rusted, was yellow-coloured; the ceiling needed redone in the room; everything had pretended luxury and been slightly shabby. There were unidentifiable scrape marks on the wall nearest the door; there had been a buzzing noise on the room's TV on the tuning of Channel 4; the carpets had been more worn than they at first seemed; the pencils, pens, stationery had been of reasonable quality only; the shampoo had been watered down; the complimentary tea and coffee brands had been unimpressive.

Penny sat back on the bed. The bed creaked.

That too, Penny thought. The bed had creaked.

(She thought it just like that, as if telling somebody about it afterwards, even though she was still actually there in the room, thinking it.)

She lay back. Hotels were such a sham. She was bored out of her mind.

She had been bored out of her mind there.

With one foot she inched the computer across the bed away from herself. Then further, further, further again until it was poised half-tipping half-balancing, right on the edge of the bed. With one hard shove she kicked it off. It fell on the floor.

She laughed.

Then it crossed her mind that it might be broken. She frowned.

Damn, she said.

But if it was broken, it might make a good story. Such as: that was the hotel I was going up to stay at when my new Powerbook got broken. Wait till I tell you how. Well. Now. It's a rough old town up there, though it seems genteel enough, the architecture and so forth. It's not that their council doesn't put a lot of money and effort into arts and things, the whole town's full of sculptures and murals, you walk through the pedestrianized area and you keep literally bumping into civic art. But, to be brutally honest, I can't say it's made any difference whatsoever.

(To whom? What? What happened, Penny? The sound of laying-down of cutlery, the slight clink of held and lifted glasses, the gathering hush of, gorgeous impatience of, satisfied throat-clearings of after-dinner listening.)

First they took my suitcase.

(They *what*? Who? Who took it?)

One of them, standing right here, as close to me as you are now, was actually rifling through my bag. All my cards were in it. Everything was in it, everything I need for my whole life.

(Penny, weren't you terrified?)

I was, completely terrified.

(How many of them were there, Penny?)

There were five. I think. But I can't really remember, it's all a bit of a blank. Anyway there wasn't another soul on the street. No cars going past, no taxis, nobody. Nothing. My worst nightmare. Honestly I can't believe what I did next.

(What? What? What did you do?)

Because my throat was dry as sand. But suddenly I heard myself say to the ringleader, this huge brute of about, I don't know, eighteen –

(Laughter.)

No, listen, listen. This is what I said, I said: If you touch me. If any of you so much as lays a *finger* on me, or on anything that's mine. And if you don't tell these thugs of yours to put my things down at once. Believe me I will bring the full weight of the law down on your head so fast that you won't know what hit you. And it'll feel like *this*.

And then I did it.

(Did it? Did what? What, Penny, what did you do?)

I hit the thug nearest to me over the head with my Powerbook.

(What? What? You did what? Laughter, incredulous female and male in-breaths.)

I really did — I hit him with the Powerbook. They're quite heavy. I can hardly believe it myself, still. You know me. I'm incapable of violence of any kind. I mean, I can't hit a fly. But there I was, and there it is. I hit him so hard that he fell down, he kind of crumpled on to his knees. And the rest of them, they took one look at him on the ground and they ran, they actually ran, they put my bag and my case down, dropped my purse on the concrete, and they all ran off and left me just standing there on the street. I mean, I had a lucky escape. Nothing was taken. And my bag was fine. My case was fine. But of course when I tried to use the Powerbook it was broken. Thousands of pounds. The weight of thousands of pounds of technology. I'd broken it over the head of a seventeen-year-old thug.

(Laughter, someone saying *knockout*, applause, congratulations, appreciative coughing.)

That was quite good, Penny thought on the bed. It wasn't flawless, but it was quite classic. It wasn't transcendent, but it would do.

(But what about the boy? one of the voices in her head interrupted as glasses clinked again and the cigarette smoke swathed itself above the table. Was he dead? Did he get up and run too? Was he left lying at your feet?)

Penny mulled over it to see which she preferred. Herself heroic and shocked and alone on a rainy street with her bags round her feet, the footsteps dying away into the rough rainy northern town. Or herself heroic and shocked and not alone at all, standing with a felled (and possibly rather pleasing-looking) boy curled and bleeding on the pedestrian walkway behind her, her sharp heels close to his eyes; then a hospital, or police, or a taxi, or his parents' house, keeping in touch afterwards, whatever, something like that. That was an adventure. That –. That was –. That could have been –.

It didn't matter what it could have been; she was finished with that story because she had leaned over and dragged the computer up on to the bed by its handle, opened it, pressed its start-up button, and it had started duly up, sprung back to life, it wasn't in the least bit broken.

But she'd lost the words she'd been typing. She hadn't saved anything. They were completely gone. Damn. She would have to start again. Fucking damning buggering shagging fuck. She hit the machine with her hand, as if the machine had been insolent to her. It rocked on the bedcovers.

Superior, she thought. She opened a new file and typed it in. Superior, yes. But she couldn't remember the others.

She could hear someone moving about and knocking on doors in the corridor outside her room.

It might be good to get out of this foul room. It might be that all she needed was outside stimulus. Someone outside this room might know another word for superior.

She rolled off the bed and opened the door.

Excuse me, she said. I was wondering.

There was someone in the hotel colour of uniform fiddling about at something over on the far wall.

Sorry, Penny said.

The person didn't turn round, was examining the wall.

Penny tried again.

Could you help me? Do you know how the TV settings work?

She went over.

Excuse me? she said.

The person jumped, turned round, backed off slightly. It was just a girl, blonde, not very old, about mid-teens, maybe sixteen Penny thought. She looked thin and dark-lidded, exactly like she should to be the ideal sixteen, and Penny found herself thinking, she's just right. Knitwear or fur skins, or something northern-urban-wintry in Lifestyle.

The girl looked cowed, like she might make a dash for the fire exit doors. Then her face got bold.

Have you anything sharp on you? she asked in an accent.

Sharp? Penny said, a little charmed. No. I'm completely unarmed.

Penny smiled. The girl didn't smile.

135

A nail file or a penknife, or something with an edge, she said.

I – um. Well, I don't know, Penny said. Wait. Wait here a minute.

Anything with an edge could do it, the girl was calling after her into the room.

Penny came back out with her make-up bag. I've these, she said. Would they do?

She handed the girl her pair of eyebrow tweezers; the girl took them and held them up so she could see their ends. Penny saw the teenage hands turning; they were unlined, pale, susceptible. She looked up. The girl was shaking her head.

Too small, she said.

Penny was disappointed. Are you sure? she said. She emptied the make-up bag on to the carpet. What about these? They're quite sharp, she said and held her nail-scissors up.

The girl took the scissors and went back over to the wall. She worked at something with the blades.

No, she said. That's too thin, that bit's too small. That's not thick enough. Have you got a two or a ten pence piece?

Oh no, I never carry money, Penny said.

The girl gave Penny a look of such irritation that Penny felt the look pass through her. Then the girl sighed, and glanced towards Penny's room. Do they give you a knife in there? she said. Or a spoon, a teaspoon, something like that?

A teaspoon? Penny said. Actually, yes, I think so. There's bound to be, isn't there? Wait a minute. Hang on.

She upended the clattering saucers and cups on the tray in her room to find the teaspoon; she brought it, triumph-ant, to the Lifestyle girl at the wall. The girl took it and peered at it. Her eyes were dark-coloured. She looked very striking. She brought her arms up and aimed the spoon, pushed one of the ends of the spoon into what Penny could see now was the head of a screw at the height of the girl's nose.

Yeah, that's quite good, the girl said.

Penny's heart lifted.

But – this bit – won't – let it go far enough – to get a hold on it, no. No.

Let me try, Penny said.

The bowl of the spoon was too sheer and too curved; its edge wouldn't fit the slot in the screw. She tried the handle end. It was too broad, it wouldn't fit at all.

Nope, Penny said. But a screwdriver would do it in a minute. You need a screwdriver.

The girl ignored her. Presumably if there had been a screwdriver downstairs she'd have brought it up with her, Penny thought. Or perhaps she'd forgotten. Perhaps she'd been sent up here to do a job and would be reprimanded if she didn't do it and was frightened to go downstairs having not done it.

Now the girl was digging at the back of the screw with the spoon.

Don't do that, Penny said. You'll hurt the, what's it called, you know. The grain. You'll break it. It'll be harder to get it out if you do.

The girl stopped immediately. For a moment Penny could actually see misery thick as velvet, luxurious, dramatic and gathered like a curtain about to fall over the girl's head. Then she blinked and the thought was gone.

Hm, Penny said. She looked at the wall instead.

There were screws holding a piece of wall on. The girl had begun to work with the end of the spoon at what Penny could now see was a thin sliver of space, paint breaking where she dug at it miserably, between the wall and the screwed-in extra piece of wall.

Something about the girl's face, how closed it was, how sure, and how peculiarly pure, made Penny want to do something, anything.

Don't, Penny said. Wait. I'll go and look. Just wait here.

This was much better. This was excellent, Penny thought as she pushed through the fire doors and skipped down the stairs. Penny had been spending another dreary night working on another publicity job in another hotel when all of a sudden quite by chance she had become a cog in the mechanism of something really happening. And if I help that girl, Penny thought as she skipped from stair to stair, that girl will always remember me as the nice person who helped her the night she was, was, doing whatever it is she's doing. And I will always remember it too, and look back on it many years from now as that night I helped the remarkable teenage chambermaid take the screws out of the wall in that hotel.

This was elating to Penny. She had come down the fire exit stairs as if the stairwell were a staircase in a film and herself the heroine coming down in her dress to the ball, everybody at the foot of it holding glasses up in the chandelier light and waiting for no one but her. She was looking (graciously, decorously, in her Southern Belle ballgown) for something sharp, or something with an edge. The fire extinguishers, no. She came back into the plushness (plushness, she thought, that's a good word, those are good words, plushness, plush) of another floor of the hotel. The framed pictures of local scenes, of cows in a field and a bridge between hills, no, nothing sharp there. The first other person she saw was a woman standing outside the door of a room, and this is how Penny came to meet, that night, one of the most interesting people she'd met in a long time, whom she took at first, completely erroneously and because of the long, rather musky, fashionable old overcoat she was wearing, to be some kind of druggy eccentric guest or maybe even a minor ex-rock star.

The woman had been looking apologetic as Penny approached, even before Penny had asked her about whether she had anything sharp. Then, after Penny had asked her twice, she shook her head.

There's something happening up on the top floor, Penny said. You don't happen to have any change handy, do you?

Uhm, the woman wearing the coat said. She looked astonished. She looked to her left and then her right. She seemed shy.

All we need is a coin, Penny said. There's a screw kind of thing in the wall, which we're trying to unscrew. We think we could unscrew it with a small coin.

Yeah? the woman said. Then she said, But some money is thinner. Than other money is.

Penny laughed, delighted by the idea of thin money. The woman stared at her, amazed.

What it is, is this, Penny said. She leaned forward, confidential. We're trying to get something off a wall, she said, as far as I can gather. The, the whatever it's called, I don't know, the slot that's cut into a screw, you know, is about this big. She held up her finger and thumb, almost touching.

The woman in the coat peered at the spacing between them.

So if you happened to have a two or a ten pence, Penny said.

Um, the woman said. She stepped away. Change jingled somewhere in her coat. Penny laughed again. Then she looked down at her feet, surprised. They were suddenly cold. Water had changed the colour of the suede of Penny's boots. The carpet beneath them was water-logged. Penny lifted one foot then the next to look at the dripping soles.

Damn, she said. These are new.

Room's, eh, leaking, the woman said.

This made Penny laugh too. The woman gaped at her, so she put her arm through the woman's arm and swung her jingling up the corridor.

Come on, she said. Come up with me, it'll be fun. It makes a change, fun at work. I'm Penny. You are?

I am what? the woman in the coat said.

Penny roared with laughter.

Have you got anything sharp? the girl turned from the wall saying to them both, for all the world as if she'd never seen Penny before, when Penny and the woman arrived out of breath on the top floor landing. Penny was a little put out.

This lady here has everything we need, she said, keeping her arm round the woman's shoulders and leading her in, because the woman in the coat had taken two steps back towards the fire doors, pulling against Penny's hold. Now she had slipped out from under Penny's arm, squatted down where she was almost as if she'd been ordered to, and began emptying handfuls of money out of her coat on to the carpet. One hand and then the other came up and out, full of change. It was astounding, Penny thought, to see so much loose change in the one place at the same time.

The woman shook her coat, felt inside the lining, dropped a last few coins.

Some of it's mine, she said.

The girl sorted through the coins with her foot. Oh yeah. A phone rang, she said.

What, my mobile? Penny said.

I don't know, the girl said. A phone in there. It rang, then it stopped.

Right, Penny said. Was it a high pitched kind of a ring? Was it, did it play a little tune kind of thing?

I don't know, for fuck sake, the girl scowled. She got up, turning money over in her hand, and went towards the wall.

Penny had decided she didn't particularly like the teenage girl. She wondered if the hotel management was aware of the attitude of some of its staff. She went back to the room and checked her mobile for messages, but there weren't any and nothing flashed on the hotel phone to suggest any message had been left for her there. She checked her wallet in her jacket pocket in the wardrobe to make sure her credit and bank cards were all still intact. She checked in her bag for her chequebook and looked inside her suitcase to see if anybody had been through anything.

Out in the corridor there was money splayed over the carpet as if part of the carpet's design.

Paint, the woman was saying.

The girl looked at Penny. What's she saying? she said.

Oh, Penny said. Don't any of them fit? She leaned down and picked up a handful of coppers. Have you tried them all? Apparently, some money is thinner than other money, did you know that?

Paint, the woman on the floor said, shaking her head. Stuck.

I can't understand what she's saying, the girl said.

Oh, Penny said. Won't they undo? What a shame. After all that.

She tried a one pence piece in one of the screws. It fitted, just, if she forced it hard, but the screw wouldn't move. She tried again. She changed the angle of her grip on the coin. It wouldn't move.

It's the paint, she told the girl. Because the screw has been painted over, it won't untwist.

The girl's face fell; it looked wild, then lost, then life went out of it. Penny began to make contingency plans. Otherwise this story would end, this evening would slip away unsolved, she'd be back in her room in a minute writing meaningless copy, and anyway Penny couldn't stand to be beaten. And it might make a good story. So she could, for instance, if she wanted to be nice (and if the teenage girl was prepared to be nice, in turn, to her) go back into the room and try the telephone directory for an all-night supermarket. If she found one, and surely they had them here, they were everywhere nowadays surely, she could ask them if they stocked power tools. If they did, she could give them a credit card number; she could give them the paper's credit card number then claim it back off expenses. She could phone a taxi service, give them the card number too and get them to deliver it plus receipt to the hotel. If there were no all-night stores, or if the all-night stores didn't stock power tools, she could ask the person at the taxi service whether any of his or her drivers owned power tools they'd drive over to the hotel at a moment's notice if she made it worth their while –

Then it moved.

The paint round it had split, making a small sound; the screw had shifted backwards a little in its spiral; the girl, tense beside her, had breathed in, ah.

Easy. Now. Let's see what else we can do, Penny said, her heart suddenly high.

Because Penny had done it, whatever it was. With a twist of each screw she broke the paint on the top four and loosened the whole top row far enough for half a (small) hand to slip behind the wall-panel. Then the girl and the woman took one side each and pulled. The girl's feet came off the ground. More paint split. Wood split. Sound split. They both fell backwards as the panel broke off the wall and fragments of snapped wood flew round them. Old air flew out, fusty. Dust flew out, hovered in the air, settled down through it to the hotel carpet.

Penny and the woman and the girl put their heads into the void.

But there's absolutely nothing there, Penny said.

Deep, the woman in the coat said. Her voice echoed a little as she leaned in. Jesus, she said. The *eep* and *ees* of what she'd said magnified round their three heads.

The girl said nothing.

Penny coughed. It was dusty. She backed out into the overhead light and saw that the wall had a gaping hole in it, black and rectangular, a space where a painting ought to be to cover it or where a wall-safe might have been blown out by outlaws. Her finger and thumb were numb at the tips, raw, red and scored where she had gripped the money and twisted the screws; the design on the money had imprinted itself in her skin. She rubbed the tips of her fingers together. She felt cheated. The panel, warped and half-broken, was leaning up against the open door of her room. She had helped take it off and behind it there had been a long shaft of nothing at all.

Penny knew she was slightly shocked. She sat down on the carpet. Shards of wood and flakes of white paint lay in among the scattered money and the eyeshadow, the eyeliner, the lip gloss out of her make-up bag. The woman in the coat was doing something with the money behind her; she could hear the soft plink of coin on coin. Penny picked up a splinter of white wood. She poked it into her finger to see what she could feel.

Nothing.

The nothing that ran the length of this hotel like a spine had appalled her.

What did you think was behind there? she asked the girl. There was panic clawing up the inside of her throat. What did they send you up here to look for? she said.

The girl was running her hand along the edge, where the wall ended and the space behind it began. Large jagged bits of wood were still screwed on where wood had broken but screws had held. They jutted out like white teeth in the mouth of the hole in the wall. The girl leaned into the hole as far as her waist and Penny was filled with the urge to catch hold of her ankles in case she fell in, but just as she was about to lunge across the room the maddening girl unbent herself out again, strolled across the hall and picked up a handful of coins. Now she was throwing coins in, one by one, dropping coins out of her hand. Money fell into the dark, inaudible.

Have either of you got a watch? the girl said. She looked from Penny to the woman then back to Penny again.

Ah, Penny said. No. Because I'm one of those people who can't wear them, listen, this is true. Whenever I put one on, whenever I have one anywhere near my body for any length of time, not just on my wrist but even if I've got it in my pocket or in a bag, if it's a digital one its numbers go completely mad, flashing and speeding up. A fuse or something blows, whatever it is inside the watch. Ordinary watches, the wind-up kind, even watches that already behave completely normally on other people's arms, won't work on mine, I had one that went so fast that it looked like I was passing whole hours while other people's watches had gone for ten or fifteen minutes. Or instead they slow down and then just break, just stop, short, never to go again, like in the children's song, you know, except that I'm not an old man, and I'm, obviously, not dead. You know, she said. My grandfather's clock, you know the old song.

Words rushed out of Penny. She explained everything. Telling them both the story had made her forget to panic. The girl waited until Penny had stopped talking, and turned to the woman in the coat.

146

Have *you* got a watch? she said.

The woman shook her head.

Penny was invisible. Then she remembered. There's a clock in my room, she said. It's in the bathroom, for some reason. I was wondering why a hotel would put a clock in the bathroom. Why? she asked the girl. Is it in case people will miss the check-out time because they're in the shower or in the bath? Anyway, if you *were* in the shower or the bath, they'd steam up, wouldn't they? The faces of them, I mean. So you wouldn't be able to read what they said. But you probably have special anti-misting fluid for cleaning the faces with.

The girl said nothing. She looked at the door of Penny's room.

Shall I go and look? Penny said.

As Penny stomped through she noticed a line left in the suede of her boots, where the wet place was drying. Damn, she said to herself. Damning buggering damn. Look at that. What I get for getting involved. Ten past nine, she shouted back through.

Has it got a third hand? the girl called.

Penny brought it out. It was a black art-deco-like clock. It had a small stylish sticker on its base, Property of Global Hotels.

It's ten past nine, she said.

The girl took it. She shook her head. She held it for a moment, turned it in her hand. Then she put her hand into the wall and dropped the clock into the hole too.

Damn, Penny thought.

First, they heard the sound of nothing at all. Then they heard the clock hitting the bottom of the shaft with a faraway plastic snap. Damn, Penny thought again. I *knew* she was going to do that.

Do you think it's broken? she said out loud.

Definitely broken, the girl said nodding, blackness under her eyes.

Do you think it was designer? Penny said.

She dared herself to the edge of the hole, dared herself to look down.

How on earth will we get it back? she said.

Dark. Nothing. A shaft of old air. She decided she'd claim that there had never been a clock. She stepped back away from the wall; it was a mess; it was nothing to do with her. If challenged she would write a letter of complaint on *World* paper saying they were charging her for something she'd never seen, the use of which she'd never had. *There was no clock in my room on the dates stated. I refuse to pay for the disappearance of something which as far as I was concerned wasn't there in the first place. I am not responsible.*

If something is missing from my room I suggest you look to your own staff for the reparation of all relevant damages and absences.

Furthermore I wish to complain about the noise and mess made by members of your staff carrying out some kind of buildings alteration programme in the corridor outside my room remarkably late in the evening for this kind of procedure on the night of my stay at your hotel.

This was disturbing not just to myself but to other guests too, and was something for which we were neither prepared nor given any apology.

The girl was talking.

But if it was heavier, she was saying, it'd fall a lot, a lot, uh, quicker. Something that weighed more would fall more quickly because it's heavier. Something, something a lot heavier, would fall faster. Would it?

Well yes, obviously it would, Penny said.

No, the woman said.

No offence. But of course it would, Penny said. Say you dropped a grand piano down that hole. That's assuming I had a grand piano available in my room to give you to drop down it, she said (pleasantly, pointedly) to the girl. Then a grand piano would obviously fall much more heavily than the clock you've just dropped down there.

A grand piano, whole, shining, falling and unassembling at the bottom of the void into sticks and strings in slowed-down motion, the flat gloss civilized surface of it crushing and splintering into cacophonic sharps, marrowbones and cleavers wavering up in the dark like broken reeds by a riverbed.

No, the woman said again.

The piano vanished in Penny's head. Penny hated to be contradicted.

The woman was piling the twos, tens, twenty pence pieces together in mounds on the carpet; she sat in a mass of silver and copper.

Galileo, she said as she sorted the money. Dropped a

149

pea and a feather off the leaning tower of Pisa. Both hit the ground at the same time.

Yes, Penny said, but if we're talking in real terms. A grand piano will fall much more heavily than a clock, a clock will fall much more heavily than a coin, a coin will fall a little more heavily than a pea –

No, the woman said again. It won't. She stopped what she was doing. She weighed different coins in her hand for a moment, then put them carefully down on top of the other coins.

Anything that gets dropped from the same place above the world, she said. It would fall at the same time. Roughly. But if they're very different shapes like a feather and a pea. Then the feather has a bit more push against the air because of its shape. But not much. But if. Imagine. If it was on the moon instead. There's no air. So a feather, a pea and even a piano. If they were all dropped above it they would reach it at exactly the same time. I mean the moon. It would be a bit slower, that's all. If it was the moon. There's only really about six times more gravity here. If it was the moon and the world you were talking about. And the things being dropped, even a piano. So small really. A piano, a pea, a feather, a coin, anything. All much the same, everything. Because what push against it that we've got here hardly counts. It makes everything as small or as big as everything else.

She stopped, and thought. Though it *would* be a lot different, she said then, if you were dropping two things at the same time and the sizes of them were, like, really

150

different. Like if you dropped something like a coin or a pea. And you dropped a planet, size of the world maybe, alongside it.

She pushed the five pence piece mound to one side. She brought the fifty pence piece pile and the pound coin pile towards herself by cupping her hands round them and began placing the coins on top of each other in columns, counting them as she did.

Penny knew the woman was wrong. She opened her mouth to say, and looked down, and she could almost see the nothing coming out of her mouth. This was a good reflex, after all; Penny wouldn't want to offend the woman in case the woman was somebody. The woman could be anybody. Who knew? It was good that she could keep quiet under pressure. But the nothing she said curled out of Penny's mouth and wound itself snake-like round her neck. It hissed; it was going to strike. Penny hated it, nothing. She hated her imagination, it was full of snakes, dead animals, and unexpectedly beautiful smashed-up pianos. This was turning into a very unpleasant evening.

Now the irritating teenage girl had peeled one of her trainers off. She went and stood by the hole she'd made in the wall. She unbuttoned her hotel uniform overall and took it off, bunched it up in her hand round the shoe. She held the things just inside the hole. The woman steadied a column of coins by her foot and watched. Penny said nothing. The girl opened her hand, let the things fall out of it. Penny wasn't sure whether she really heard them land or imagined she did, the trainer with the muffled thud of rubber, the uniform more airy with a light material sigh.

The girl slid down to the floor, leaning against the wall. She looked exhausted. She looked about to cry.

The woman in the coat stood up. She took half of one of the columns of pound coins and some of the smaller change, and let it all fall into the insides of her coat again. The noise it made was jarring.

You know, she said. That they keep Big Ben in London running with two pence pieces? They pile them on the pendulum. That makes it keep the right time.

She gestured first to the hole in the wall, then to the sorted money on the carpet. Yours, she said to the girl. Thirty-two pounds fifty. Minus what you dropped in there.

She stepped over the money and nodded to the girl and then to Penny. Hands in her pockets, she pushed through the stair doors. They swung shut stiff on their hinges behind her.

Penny felt utterly abandoned. Worse, the girl had started, noiselessly, to cry. She had put her head down inside her arms, was rocking slightly, back and fore on the floor. Penny got up. One of the girl's feet, small without its shoe, had skin that was bare and white just above the ankle sock.

Don't, Penny said, from where she stood. Oh, don't cry. Please don't. It's all right. It'll be all right.

The girl rocked and cried. Penny looked round, uneasy. She could just go into her room and shut the door. But the

teenage girl would still be crying out here and Penny, on
the other side of nothing more than a thin door, would
know (and worse, would maybe still be able to hear it).
Or she could go into her room and call another member
of staff. Then that other member of staff could come
upstairs and be responsible for this member of staff.

Penny picked up the cracked wood panel and carried it
away from her door across to a door on the far side of the
lobby. She leaned it up against someone else's room. She
checked both her hands carefully for splinters. She bent
down and picked her make-up out of the money and
debris. She put things back into the make-up bag. She
blew paint flakes off her make-up mirror and wiped it
clean on a clean patch of carpet.

Back in her own room she pressed the number 1 on her
phone. She meant well.

Hello, Reception, a voice said.

Hello, Penny said. This is Room 34. A member of your
staff seems to be crying in the corridor outside my door.

Penny pulled her coat on. She slipped the strap of her
bag on to her shoulder. She shut the door behind her and
tested it to make sure it was locked. She stepped over the
piles of coins and crossed the hall. She pressed the lift
button and stood waiting for the lift doors to open. The
lift took a long time.

From over by the lift doors she called to the girl,
crosslegged and weeping, leaning against the disfigured
wall. The hollow socket of it sagged open above the girl's
head.

Someone's on their way up, Penny said in a cheery voice. Won't be long now.

At the bottom of the shaft, colourless in the dark, there was a shoe and a crumpled uniform, both still warm, both going cold. There were three or four coins, maybe more. There was a broken clock. Its plastic shell was shattered and its face was in bits.

A bell pinged. The lift door opened. Penny got in. The lift door closed.

She put her weight against the revolving door and pushed it round till she found herself on the street. Relief streamed over her, unheated unconditioned air. She had been blessed with the gift of no guilt, or at least the gift of guilt that was never more than momentary, a matter of the imagination only. All she ever had to do was change her air. She stood in the hotel doorway and breathed in, then out again.

It had stopped raining. Penny could see the woman in the coat ahead of her, slowly crossing the road. She caught up with her outside a warehouse. The woman was looking in its window, using her hand to shade her eyes so she could see in beyond the reflective streetlight. Penny looked in too. She saw herself superimposed on rolls of cheap carpeting.

Hello again, Penny said.

The woman saw her, ignored her, carried on peering into the warehouse.

There was a story here somewhere. Penny could sense

it, feel it, as if half-remembered. She was on to something.
She persevered.

God knows what all that was about, she said.
Cigarette?

The woman shook her head.

I can't bear it when people cry, Penny said. She lit up,
breathed smoke in, blew smoke out. But luckily I was
born with the gift of no guilt, she said. What are you
going to do now? Where are you off to, anywhere
interesting?

The woman shrugged.

Do you want to go for a drink somewhere, Penny said,
something to eat?

The woman turned away, said something garbled. It
sounded like she said she was going to look at the horses.

I'll come, Penny said. I love horses.

The woman laughed, choked, coughed. She shook her
head and held herself. Houses, she said when she'd
stopped coughing.

Oh, Penny said. Houses, right. Well, can I chum you
along? To be honest with you, I've absolutely nothing else
to do, at least for the next while.

The woman's face was expressionless. After a moment
she nodded.

She led the way down the side of the warehouse then
along a badly lit road, deserted except for three cars
slewed outside a Chinese takeaway.

Are you looking at houses to buy a house? Penny said.

Uh? the woman said.

I was just wondering if you're looking at houses because you're hoping to buy one, Penny said.

The woman wheezed another coughing laugh. Yeah, she said. That's right.

They walked past some boys sitting and leaning on the takeaway wall. Hello, Penny said as they passed. *Hello*, the boys mimicked. One of them threw something after Penny and the woman. It was a flattened beercan. The boys fell about laughing, shouted something else. Bye, Penny shouted. *Bye*, they shouted back.

The woman was limping. For someone with a limp she moved fast and Penny was under pressure keeping up with her.

Have you hurt yourself? Pulled a muscle? Penny said.

Yeah. Playing tennis, the woman said.

You have to be careful with tennis, Penny said. You have to stretch well beforehand otherwise you can do yourself real damage.

The wind blew. They walked for what felt like miles. The woman stopped often to cough. After a couple of tries Penny stopped talking; the silence back made her embarrassed. The coughing made her wince inside. It was possible the woman was an alcoholic. It was all nearly as embarrassing as the crying girl had been. She began to regret leaving the hotel and to think about turning back while she could still remember the way. But if she turned back, she'd have to pass those boys outside the takeaway, by herself this time. Possibly she hadn't left it long enough yet for the hotel people to sort out the crying. So they passed from the town into a suburb of the town and the scent on the wind changed from winter-damp metal to winter-damp earth, the smell of hedges and strips of garden. There were rose-bushes dug into the middles of small front lawn after small front lawn; they were bare, or the roses on them were frostbitten.

The woman stopped.

They were outside a window with its curtains open; they could see in. A child, a girl, sat on a sofa reading a book. A woman came into the room, said something. The child rolled her eyes and put the book down. She left the room, shutting a door behind her.

You like this one? Penny said, looking at the house. It was mid-terrace. It was squat and ugly. It would surely be worth little. There was open grass in a square in front of it with several cars parked on it. One had no windscreen.

Shh, the woman said. Or maybe it was just the noise her breathing was making, Penny couldn't be sure. She stood in front of the window a little longer. Then she started walking again.

She stopped by another lit window several houses down. Penny caught up. Behind this one a man was standing on a chair trying to watch television while a woman measured his legs with a tape-measure.

Do you know them? Penny asked. The woman shook her head. She looked at Penny and her look was fierce; Penny stepped back, alarmed. Behind the window the man had said something which made the woman inside laugh. She laughed as though her lips were holding pins.

He laughed too. She took the pins out of her mouth, held them away from herself in her hand and sank to the floor laughing.

Just when it was getting interesting, when the people had stopped laughing behind the glass and were falling into each other's arms on the floor, the woman in the coat moved on. Each time they found a window whose curtains were open and whose lights were on, the woman stopped outside it and stood by the gate where she could see. From terrace to terrace, house to harled house with garden after small square garden, their windows too small as if shrunken, the light behind their drawn curtains making squares of tawdry colour in the night, the rooms Penny could see into were full of unlikeable furniture. Repetitious armchairs angled in corners towards corners; worthless stuff piled up or neat, familial, claustrophobic, on shelves and mantelpieces. People in the lit rooms watched televisions, or televisions blared fast-moving light into empty rooms with windows uncurtained open to the dark, and the houses went on forever. There were unmowed grass edgings in front of them, and between their pavements and the roads. It was municipal grass. Penny walked on the pavement. She took care not to walk on the grass at all.

The woman was watching more people watching television again. Penny shuffled, put her hands up her sleeves, made cold noises. Brr, she said. The woman flinched; her held-up hand told Penny to be quiet again.

Penny went over to lean against a lamppost; she was

angry. She opened her bag under the light of it to see if she
had any paracetamol with her. She didn't. She was getting
a chill. She was getting a headache. It was fucking buggering damnably freezing. They passed from a rough street,
the houses patched or boarded and the gardens dog-
chewed, into a richer set of streets where the cars were in
better shape and the gardens full of cut-back clematis and
winter pansies recently planted.

This is a much nicer place to buy, Penny whispered,
confidential.

The woman was staring in at a middle-aged woman
wearing a bathrobe, drinking something out of a mug and
eating something orange off a plate. Occasionally she
glanced down at a newspaper on her lap, other than that
she gazed ahead of her. There was no light flickering.
Possibly she was listening to music, or the radio. Possibly
she was sitting in a silent room. Penny memorized the
name of the road up on one of the walls of a house on a
corner. It would be okay, slightly better, to take a taxi
from round here. But she had taken her mobile out of her
bag and left it at the hotel, it was still next to the hotel
phone, and she had no money with her to call a taxi with.
Christ, Penny thought. Damn. Her heart sank. She
panicked.

But the woman in the coat had money with her, she had
plenty of change, Penny knew this, she had seen her put it
in her pocket on the hotel landing. Her heart rose. There
would be a callbox somewhere. And if Penny was
somehow left on her own here, anywhere around here (it

sank), she could always reverse the charges to someone at home or at the paper and have them call a taxi for her through Talking Pages (it rose again), who could find numbers for anywhere in the country regardless of where you were phoning from.

They crossed a grass embankment, Penny lagging behind, worrying all the way across it about whom exactly to phone. Then she began worrying for her boots. On the other side, in a street of pleasant semi-detached villas, a clean-looking elderly lady wandered about in the middle of the road between the lines of parked cars.

Hello, Penny said. We're out looking at houses. Aren't you cold?

The elderly lady wasn't wearing a coat. She told Penny she was looking for her cat.

She's never been out this late, the elderly lady said. I just turned around and she was gone. It's not like her. I don't know what to do.

Don't worry, Penny said. Have you checked all round your house? She might be asleep in a cupboard or under a bed. Cats are very independent. They can look after themselves. Go inside, it's cold. She'll come home by herself. She's probably there now.

She's black and white, the elderly lady said. Have you seen her?

No, Penny said.

She has a white spot here above her eye and a white bib. She never goes out. She must have slipped out when the lifeboat people knocked on the door. She must have gone out when I went to get my purse. I never let her out. She never goes out.

The woman in the coat had gone, limped far in the distance, was turning a corner. Penny couldn't believe how far. She panicked again. She said goodbye to the elderly lady who didn't hear her, was bending to look underneath a car. Penny ran to keep up. The heels of her boots slowed her down. Ahead of her, the woman disappeared, hunched and limping, over a railway bridge.

Finally Penny found her sitting on a bench made of concrete outside what looked like a small shopping centre. Behind her was a library and a couple of shops. One was a shoe shop and had Christmas decorations round the shoes in its window. The other had been emptied and closed-up; its window was dark, bare apart from a banner which said 50% OFF EVERYTHING; its insides were stripped. Its sign said: Hiltons Simply The Best. Penny couldn't work out from what was left of it what it was that the shop used to sell. It depressed her. She turned to look in the opposite direction. In the distance there was a racketing noise; she could see two boys on skateboards throwing themselves against concrete slopes behind the shops.

That'll keep them nice and warm, Penny said.

The woman's face was deep down inside her coat. Her breath came out of a gap between two buttons.

There was a public phone in the front alcove of the shut library. Penny's heart rose again. She went over, picked up the receiver. It worked. God. Thank God. That was a blessing. It was almost time to ask politely, don't you think we should maybe call a taxi now to get us back to the hotel? It's so cold, and I have to get back now. I've got to work when I get in, it's been a lovely walk, thank you. But when she sat down on the bench beside the woman for a moment and started to say it, the wind blew a hair into her open mouth. It wasn't her own hair, or the woman in the coat's. It was long. It was someone else's entirely. Penny picked it out, disgusted. Then she held it up in front of her. Its ends blew about.

In a way it was the same, she thought, exactly the same, as watching through the windows of all those houses had been, seeing people who had no idea that anyone was watching them. The women sewing, leaning on their hands, and the TV pictures flickering like open fires in their sitting rooms. The men delicately placing cigarettes between their lips, or asleep, network light shifting on their faces. The endless eating and drinking; she had been watching the eating process all night from outside unknowing people's houses. Think of it. People, if they'd looked up and out, at the square of black they made by leaving the curtains open or the blinds up in their rooms, would have seen, not black at all, and certainly not people watching them there, but themselves, reflected in the reflections of the rooms they lived in. If they'd switched their lights off, let their eyes adjust to the change, then looked out again, what would they have seen outside their houses? Whom would they have seen? Would they have seen anyone there at all?

It was foul and it was queasily exciting, this humdrum digestive-system exotica of others' lives; Penny was repelled and energized by it, the knowledge that she could be brought together with someone else by the simple flick of a switch from light to dark, or by a literal thread, by something with the thinness, the genetic randomness, the intimacy of a single hair from a single other head. She held the long hair up in the wind. She let it go. It blew off her glove and she followed it with her eyes along the pavement as far as she could before it disappeared. She turned to let herself take a good look for the first time at the woman sitting shivering next to her on this bench made of cold stone.

The woman looked tired out. Her breathing was short and audible, as if she were breathing through several layers of wet material. Every breath she breathed was shadowed by another separate breath somewhere at the back of it. She looked like she had already been savaged by something stronger than she was. There was something about her; obliqueness in the eyes, tautness around the mouth, deliberation in the way of sitting, all of which suggested she had been unplugged, she was running on back-up power, a kind of energy that was finite. Her hands were closed but their closedness was submissive, her boots hung on the end of her legs as if they might belong to someone else. How she sat, how she moved, how she walked, slumped and alert, frozen and careless at once, was telling. Penny tried to think what of. Partly she was dead to the world. Partly there was something about her that was more commanding than anyone Penny could at this precise moment in time think of, and it struck Penny for the first time that she had met, in the course of her life so far, literally thousands of other people, none of whom had been at all like this one.

She decided she'd give things another few minutes out here before she went back to the hotel. You never knew what could happen. This was one of the things she liked about herself, that she was so open to experience, to experiences like this one.

She waited politely until the woman had stopped coughing. She took her cigarettes out of her bag again, and then she began.

Sure I can't tempt you? Penny said.

Bad for you, the woman said.

Don't mind if I do? Penny said.

The woman shook her head.

What's your name? Penny asked as she lit her own. What do you do?

Do? the woman said.

You know, Penny said. To live.

Ah, live, the woman said. Her voice, gravelled, came from inside her coat. Penny waited, but the woman didn't say anything else.

Cold tonight, Penny said.

Clear, the woman said. She gestured up.

Above them the sky was acned with stars. Lovely, Penny said. She shivered. She tried another tack.

What do you think she was doing, that maid in the hotel? she asked again.

The woman shrugged again.

Penny eyed the public telephone behind the woman's shoulder, but then the woman said something.

She needed to take that wall apart, she said.

Yes, Penny said. She seemed lost, a lost thing. I think she was actually too young to have been working. I was thinking of checking up on it when we get back. What do you think?

She isn't a runaway, the woman said.

Penny nodded blankly.

It was her money, the woman said.

Ah, Penny said, bewildered. Now I'm lost too, she said.

Yeah, the woman said. It's good. That way, you're probably not still going to get it.

Get what? Penny said.

Lost, the woman said.

Oh *right*, Penny said. Lost. I see.

If you know you are, the woman said. Then you're not about to be it, lost.

Penny memorized that. If you know you're lost then you're probably not just about to get lost. Was that it? She wasn't sure. Clever, she said out loud.

The woman nodded.

Then she said, See that old woman on Morgan Road? Did she tell you she'd lost her cat?

Poor thing, Penny said. I hope she found it.

No, the woman said. She's always out looking for a cat.

There isn't one. If there was ever a cat, it went months ago.

Oh, Penny said. Do you often do the walk we did tonight, then? Do you stay up here often?

I don't think there is a cat, the woman said.

Penny knew that some people like to live in hotels rather than have a house or rent a place. Do you live over in the hotel? she asked.

Silence.

Penny stubbed out her cigarette on the stone arm of the bench. She thought she'd try, just once more, one more time.

You're not from here originally, are you? she said.

The woman shook her head.

Where did you grow up, then? Penny said.

The woman breathed, saying nothing.

It's funny, Penny said, as though talking to herself. When people ask me that kind of thing, I usually tell whoever asked me a lie. You know, a white lie. I tell them that my childhood was miserable, and that I'm an orphan. Can you still be an orphan in your thirties? I used to tell people who asked me, at parties or wherever. I'd say, *actually I'm an orphan*, and watch their faces, it was kind of fun, seeing such immediate discomfort. In the long run I think it makes people imagine I've come through something extraordinary, something which at some point they have to experience for themselves, both parents dead. And at the same time it makes them see me as vulnerable, needing special care. Perfect combination. But to be honest for once in my life, Penny said. Which I rarely am.

Penny checked. The woman seemed to be listening. Penny went on.

My mother and father are actually both still quite happily alive. Well, to tell the truth, quite gloomily and miserably alive. They live in different cities now, which makes Christmas a little tricky for my brother and I. They're both well-off. We were brought up in reasonable comfort. My childhood was averagely happy, averagely tortured. And since I'm being honest with you, this is how it went. My father had affairs with women who weren't my mother. Most fathers do. So when I was a teenager, and I realized this was what he was doing, I started what you might call taking things. You know, from shops. From other people's houses too but mainly from shops.

The woman still seemed to be listening.

I took everything I could, from everywhere I could. It's remarkably easy to do. I kept all the things under my bed; I think they're all still there in my teenage bedroom at my father's house. I was particularly good at hair accessories; they're easy to slip up your sleeve, easy, a whole handful of them in their packets off a rack and into a bag or up a sleeve. They're all still there under the bed, hordes of them, little plastic balls and elasticated things, all still in their packaging. Make-up, little computer games. Occasionally I get something out from under there and have a look at it, when I'm staying at my father's house. Clothes too. Skirts, jumpers, tops. It's like a dated treasure trove under there. Everything is pink, grey, light blue, pastel-coloured, woefully old-fashioned now when I look at it again. I took cups out of people's kitchens, or spoons, whatever. I used to dare myself to leave whatever house we visited with whatever I could take.

It hadn't worked yet. Now the mother, Penny thought.

My mother, she said, always preferred my brother to me. I know that, I knew it. I don't mind now. There was a time when I did mind, and I took it out on her without her knowing by, well, sex really, I started sleeping with an old friend of hers and my father's. I saw him at a station one day on the outskirts of London. He used to come to our house, I knew him. He was a kind of father figure, you know how it is.

The woman nodded at last. Hooked, Penny thought and felt the thrill of it, slight chill on the back of her neck.

I thought, that's what I'll do. And I did it, we had very rushed sex in the empty station waiting room. My first time. It was all quite exciting. All quite seedy. Terrible. You know?

The woman looked at Penny, sympathetic. Penny looked dolefully back. Sex, she thought behind the doleful face. If the stealing doesn't do it, and the my-parents-didn't-understand-me, then the sex, the sex always does.

She carried on talking.

I used to wear very short skirts for him, he liked it. I used to steal short skirts especially. I was seventeen. He ran a newspaper. In fact he gave me my first job on a paper. So I suppose that experience marked my life for good, in more ways than one.

The woman moved suddenly beside Penny. A paper? she said. Like a newspaper?

The *World*, Penny said. It's full of grey space. Since I'm being truthful. We have to fill it up as fast as we can. That's what I do. That's my job, filling up the grey space every week for people like you and me.

She nudged the woman, like they were friends. The woman shook her head. Do you not work on a paper, then? she said.

I work on the *World*, Penny said. The *World*. You know. The *World on Sunday*.

Is that a paper? the woman said.

The *World*, Penny said again.

Is it a, I forget the word for it, the woman said. She put her arms out, as if holding something too big for her.

Penny laughed. I can't believe you don't know the *World*, she said. But the woman's eyes had widened and her head had come right out of her coat.

Are you a journalist? she said. You interview people and stuff?

Well, mostly just people, Penny said. Stuff isn't usually very forthcoming.

Was it your paper who did that page? the woman was saying. She was waving her hands about. Penny sat back.

Probably, she said. Which?

The page, the one about what was in the pockets of homeless people, what people kept in their pockets?

Um, Penny said.

There would have been a photograph in it of the things

in the person's pockets. It would have been all laid out for a photograph. And then there would have been a written thing about the person too, the woman said. Their name, where the picture was taken, things like that.

No, I don't think I remember a piece like that, Penny said. Not while I've been with the *World*.

Is it long that you've been with the *World*? the woman said.

Well, three years there now, Penny said.

The woman's eyes clouded. Oh, she said, and turned away. Then she turned back again. But do you remember a page like that, from any other paper, did you ever see it? she asked.

Nope, Penny said shaking her head. Certainly not in our *World*. Other people still do that kind of story. It was probably somewhere else, we aren't doing many just now. To be frank with you they don't make good copy; with the last government it was always a good injustice story or a good humane story. With this government it just looks like whining. Nobody's really doing them any more. Unless there's a drug element. Drug stories are still okay.

There *is* a drug element, the woman said. Everyone takes them. Everyone on the street takes stuff, we all do.

You all do, Penny said.

You have to, the woman said. Fucks with your brain, I mean really really fucks it. Sorry about the swearing, she said, as a kind of afterthought.

That's what you do, Penny said.

And also, the woman said. It really changes people.

On the street, Penny said again.

Yeah, wherever, the woman said. It can really make people into ugly fuckers.

The woman stopped. She sat, said nothing. She shook her head. She held her hands up, open, empty. Then she said, Sorry again. Language.

I'm an idiot, Penny was thinking. I'm such an idiot. Look. The coat. The money. The bad skin, the smell, the listless readiness. The wandering about. The breathing. I'm such a fool. The penny had dropped. Penny Drops. A good heading. It made her want to laugh again. Then it made her think of the public phone, and a taxi, and a warm room, with curtains, shut.

The woman was talking. I'm sorry? Penny said.

Things, the woman said. If you touch them, like. Ruined.

You know, Penny said. Earlier when we met, I thought you had a room in the hotel.

Yeah, the homeless woman said. I did.

Oh, Penny said. She stood up now, was stamping her feet. Her boots were ruined and her feet were frozen. She wondered if she'd ever feel her feet again.

Is it news and historic things like that air war there was that you report on? the homeless woman said.

Mm? Penny said. Oh no, I do the style pages, she said. Though once, for one article, I had to jump out of a plane. That was fun.

Wow, right, the woman said politely.

Penny walked into the middle of the road. Cars went

171

past, but none were taxis. Do taxis ever come out here? she called. She stamped her ruined boots.

Can I maybe ask you a favour? the woman said.

Mm? Penny called from the middle of the road, where she was wondering whether taxis up here would take credit cards or not.

A favour. Can I ask you a meaning?

How do you mean, a meaning? Penny said coming back on to the pavement.

There's a word. I don't know what it means, the woman said.

Uh-huh? Which word? Penny asked, stamping her heels, looking down the road for signs of other life.

Rebiggot, the woman said.

Penny stopped. Re-what? she said.

The woman spelt the word out. Penny shook her head.

I don't know, she said. I don't know what that word means. It's not a word I'm familiar with at all.

It's out of a poem, the woman said. I am rebiggot.

Penny opened her bag. She found her pen and looked for something to write on. The woman spelt the word again, and Penny wrote it letter by letter on the inside cover of her chequebook. She held it under what light there was from the shut library, shook her head.

Nope, Penny said. Never heard of it. It looks foreign. French? Sorry.

Penny surprised herself by actually feeling it, sorry. She looked at the woman again. She thought how the woman had been so wrong, how she'd even believed there was gravity on the moon. Everyone knew there wasn't. She smiled to herself. She carried on writing in her chequebook.

What's your name? she asked the woman again. Tell me your name, please. I've had a lovely time tonight with you. It's made a real difference to me, meeting you tonight.

The woman looked pleased.

Elspeth, she said.

Elspeth. Elspeth what? Penny said, still writing.

What do you want to know it for? the woman said.

I just want to know. So I remember, Penny said.

The woman thought for a moment. Then she said, Freeman. Elspeth Freeman.

Penny Warner, Penny said. Pleased to have met you. She pulled off her glove and held out her hand. The woman, surprised, pleased, took Penny's warm hand in her own cold one.

Now, Elspeth, Penny said. If you ever need anything.

Penny slipped the folded cheque inside the woman's coat pocket, tucked it in, patted it. She forgot about her ruined boots. Her heart rose, flew about; her heart was like a bird, ecstatic, high above her head.

And one last thing, she said. Do you need a lift back to the hotel?

The homeless woman shook her head.

Okay. So do you know where there's a taxi rank round here? Penny said. Or could you, possibly, Elspeth, let me borrow, would it be possible for you to lend me, some change for that phone over there, so I can call a taxi? I've got to get back. Work to do.

The woman had already put her hand deep inside the lining of her coat, she had brought out a twenty pence piece, she was holding it up.

Here you are, she said.

By the time she was back at the hotel Penny had become anxious about having written a cheque for so much. By the time the lift had reached her floor she had decided what to do about it.

The lift door opened. Penny peeked out.

The girl was gone. All the loose change was gone. The hall had been tidied up. But the gash in the wall was still there, horrible. Penny put her head at an angle so as not to see it. She unlocked her door. In her room, clear and plastic, was the smell of new computer.

Nice, she thought.

She drew the curtains shut, kicked off her stained, spoiled boots and flopped herself on to the bed.

Tired, she thought.

There were no messages for her on either phone. She started the computer up. Its clock said 11:15 p.m. There were no e-mails waiting. For a moment she felt bereft. Then she typed her opening paragraph straight out. She read it over. It needed almost nothing else.

Good, she thought.

She reached for the phone and dialled 1.

Hello, Reception, a voice said.

Hello, Penny said, this is Room 34. I'd like a Club Sandwich.

Certainly madam, the voice said. I'll connect you to Room Service.

And one other thing, Penny said. Can you tell me the combination for pay-per-view for this room? I can't find the information anywhere in the room. I've been looking all evening.

Certainly madam, the voice said. As it says inside our Global Information Brochure under the heading Pay-Per-View, you just double your room number. So your pay-per-view combination, for instance, since you're in Room 34, will be 3434.

Ah, Penny said.

Room Service? a voice said.

This is Room 34, Penny said. Can you send me up a Club Sandwich?

Certainly madam, the voice said. Would you like anything to drink with your order?

Hot chocolate, Penny said.

Certainly madam. With cream?

No, Penny said.

Penny hung up. She pressed the on button on the remote, and reeled through the channels until she found the crypted-over channel from earlier in the evening. She keyed in her number. Words on the screen told her to press the button marked *BUY*. Penny pressed it. The channel decrypted immediately. A woman in a fedora and an unbuttoned mac was sitting in a car outside a house.

175

She was clearly supposed to be a private detective; she carried a camera with a ridiculously long lens. Through the lens she was watching a man and a woman having sex in a kitchen. She watched them, then she put the camera down and put a finger into her mouth. The woman having sex moaned. She held on to the sideboard. The man talked in a quiet voice. He turned the woman round on the table and went in from behind. The woman moaned some more. Her head was next to a block of knives, a plate covered in what looked like uncooked bacon and a basket of cakes with white icing and red cherries on top. The man wrapped some of the bacon round his index finger and looked as if he were about to poke it inside the woman's anus. The camera cut to the woman in the car, who had taken the lens off the camera and had put it between her legs. Ooh, she said. She moved backwards and forwards on the lens inside the car.

Penny finished her second paragraph and read it out to herself.

Great, she thought.

Then she remembered, and got her chequebook out. There was a word written on it. It was the word the homeless woman had wanted to know. Half-curious, Penny called up Spellcheck on her computer screen and typed in the letters r e, then b e g, then o and t, but the Spellcheck came up blank. After a moment it suggested replacing the word with the word *reboot*. She tried the Thesaurus. *The word was not found*, the Thesaurus told her. *Choose another word to look up*. It listed the following words instead: rebel, rebellion, rebelliousness, rebirth, rebuild, rebuff.

The Room Service order came.

Penny signed for it, ate it and drank it.

She thought over the evening as she ate. It hadn't been dull. It had been unexpectedly interesting. Nobody would believe she had been for a walk round the worst areas in town looking into people's houses with a homeless person who had asked her the meanings of words. Would anybody be that interested? But she had liked the homeless woman, who had taken her to see front gardens, one with an old sofa in it, one with a fridge, gardens with children's toys abandoned in them, or with fuchsias and roses and perfectly edged black lawns in them. The Garden of England. Blair's Britain at the Dawn of New Millennium kind of thing. She should suggest it. She would work on it. Thought-provoking, kitsch value, old-fashioned class value as well as social value. She was pleased. The night had given her a great deal she hadn't expected.

She wondered if the homeless woman had been casing the houses for anything valuable.

Before she forgot again, she dialled 24-Hour Banking and keyed in her pass-numbers. She told the man the number of the cheque.

Cancelled? the man said.

Penny paused. Something made her freeze as surely as if someone somewhere had aimed a remote control at her and pressed the button with the word *pause* on it. In the frozen moment she remembered: the width and

177

narrowness of money; the great clock towering the Thames and the Houses of Parliament, its pendulum kept in order by a pillar of small coins; a man with a beard climbing uneven steps holding in the dip of his hand a feather and a pea; and the way that the borrowed money had fallen inside the callbox so that someone at the other end of a phone could say something and she would be heard by them.

Hello? the man on the phone said. Hello?

Then she was back in the hotel room, sitting on the bed holding the receiver and talking to someone she didn't know in a bank that never closed.

Please, she said.

For a minute there she thought she'd gone soft. For a minute there, the universe had shifted. But no. Good. As she read out the last two numbers of the cheque, she felt it; crude to put it like this, perhaps, with what had happened outside her door earlier that evening, and what was happening on the hotel television screen right in front of her, right then. But something inside her which had been forced open had sealed up again. Good, she thought again, pleased with herself first for the initial extravagance of her act, and next for being able to, crucially being sensible enough to, put a stop to it. If you were poor, you were poor. You couldn't handle money. Money was nothing but a problem if you weren't used to it. It must be a relief, to have none. It was no accident that the words poor and pure were so alike.

Homeless Woman Windfall. Penny From Heaven.

She laughed. That was good. She was firing on all cylinders. She wrote the last paragraph of the hotel piece and read through the whole thing.

That, she thought, will do nicely.

Wary of calling down for someone to fold her covers back (in case they sent up that girl from earlier in the hall) she rolled them back herself. She checked the sheets, like she always did, for cigarette burns, bloodspots, marks of any kind, hairs.

She had finished the piece, had saved it and had sent it down the line. She had left the television on, low-volume fleshy creaking in the background, and the lights on too. (Usually this kept it at bay, but tonight she would dream again of falling out of the plane, the pack on her back faulty, the straps and ropes tangled and the chute not opening as she falls above the lonely rolling English countryside, trees below her so small that she could pick one up between her finger and thumb and put it on her tongue like an international delicacy she isn't sure of the correct way of eating. But what if someone has seen her eat it incorrectly, and what if the tree in her stomach swells as she falls to its actual size like the trees below her, her stomach about to burst open, leaves and branches and trunk and roots come furiously new-born out of her?) She had the hotel shampoo, the hotel stationery, the hotel pen, the hotel pencil, the hotel cotton buds, the hotel shoewipe, the hotel handcream, all packed away in her case for her early start back down south tomorrow.

She stretched herself out in the bed. It was huge. It was

sweet-smelling. It was warmed-up from where she'd been lying on it. She was about to fall far, deep, fast, asleep.

Perfect, she thought as she did.

WORLD HOTELS

It doesn't matter where you are in the world if you're anywhere near a Global Hotel. You could be, literally, anywhere. You could even be home. For work, for relaxation, for the ideal get-away-from-it-all, and for stylish, spacious bedrooms whose unique individual design is just one of the classy hallmarks of the Global Hotel phenomenon, you can't beat them. They're good.

Why go there?

Who needs an excuse? These relaxed, informal, usually small hotels in the very hip and trendy Global category are their own raison d'être. Affordably priced, elegantly adapted, they're miles ahead of the guest-house competition when it comes to leaving nothing to be desired.

Why stay there?

Because you won't be able to help it! New York, Brussels, Leeds, wherever, we practically guarantee you that if you're in a Global the temptation will be to spend your whole holiday (like we did) in your room, revelling in the lush, plush settings they do so well. You'll be so perfectly at home in whatever armchair you've happened to fall into that you'll find it hard to get out of the chair, never mind the room. And the food! Don't get us started on the food. Another reason you won't want to go out. Global makes a point of hiring seasoned, fashionable chefs who cook up such a bill of fare that wherever you are you're eating at a Capital-City-high standard.

City life

Excellent for business meetings and pretty well equipped for everyone from the lone traveller to the full-scale small conference, we found the seductive Global rates are probably well worth a look whatever your needs might be.

Winter weekends

Let's face it, winter is hard work, hard winds, hard going. Or – alternatively – you could be enjoying a luxurious soak, enjoying the comfort of flawless staff attention, enjoying blissing out to the latest in TV technology in your room, or just blissing out to a room with a Global view. Why not let yourself get utterly oblivious? High on style, low on fuss, and the perfect hideaway, the classic yet contemporary Global will provide an environment that's hard to better. A transcendent time is ready and waiting to be had by all.

World Perfect awards the Global chain nine out of ten. Effortless style and an effortless visit.

A superior stay.

future in the past

& since the main thing is I counted I was there
& since I have come home with really the most fucking
amazing new shoes & also they gave me the breakfast &
it was really good
& since there is the five pound note
& since I knew I did know already about the horrible
thing about being crammed-in all upside down I had read
it in the papers it wasn't a surprise or a shock or anything
I did know
& since she was fast since she was so incredibly fast I
bet she'd be pleased I'm sure she'd be pleased how fast
I like to think she is light as air lighter than it now like
those pictures they take of car headlights in cities where
the cars are going too fast to leave anything of themselves
but their lights as they go so fast past the camera it is like
that with her I am sure I think she could go round town
all day & all night if she wanted at a really amazing
stream of light & speed over the tops of the buildings she
could even dive out of the high windows of that hotel she
would just float she wouldn't fall she wouldn't have to
because now she can tread air too not just water like
people who are only alive well that's what I think anyhow
& since usually at this time of the night no not really

night morning really what time is it half past four since
at this time of the morning it is me staring at the airtex in
the ceiling & it all going round in circles in my head me
going over & over it that she was going to she was to
have gone up to maybe even sub in the national team
they said they would maybe test her for the team that
sometimes subs for the national team if she could have
got her time on the butterfly right she needed to shave it
she said to not quite half a second less that's what she
told me that they were on the point of offering it to her if
she could make it a 0.45 of a second faster she was saying
it she was in bed right there right over there she would be
able to go for the trials they told her she was still fast for
her age if she could do the 0.45 thing 0.45 of a second it
is nothing it is like almost nothing no time at all like that
that that that that past you so fast you can hardly tell it
was even there that was all she needed to lose off her time
to shave it she said & she hadn't told anyone in case it
didn't happen because she said it might jinx it I haven't
told anybody I haven't told a soul sub that means sub-
stitute imagine Sara my sister Sara Wilby might have
been a sub for a national team that is fucking amazing
really & she her voice was just there inches away over
there I could have reached my hand out imagine if you
shaved a butterfly that would be terrible you would have
to be careful what if you sliced through something its
antennae its proboscis where would you shave it there's
nowhere to there's no extra on a butterfly it was the
Wednesday night she was right there telling me & it was

weird because usually she never told me anything she never usually said anything to me about anything & then after that it was on the Monday night after that that was the Monday night she never came home when she was supposed to she never came   every night ever since then since that night it has been the bits of her coming at me like they are all demanding I never know what & it's like say she was standing there at the end of my bed & then she suddenly flew apart she just fell apart small bits of her her ear neck the hollow of her neck hand fingers toes her heel her foot the bit where her swimsuit dipped down & the shoulderblade in it eye mouth muscles her oh God fuck sake it makes me weird in my stomach the word the breast like it stares at me some nights looking at me with like just its one open eye sometimes there's two of them two eyes like staring like when he says I am being really insolent well Sara you have a really fucking insolent chest well you had God I am weird I am fucking gone I tell you I am a lobotomic case anyway not yet tonight it hasn't come still all the same I still can't get to sleep maybe after tonight I think because it has made my heart go so fast or maybe it is all the food they gave me at the hotel I ate a lot I haven't eaten as much as that for God ages now I don't know how long kind of forgot about food really

& since now I know for sure though really I knew already that she didn't actually mean to do it I suppose that too is keeping me awake though more usually at this time of the night morning I am lying here not sleeping again because I am thinking all that stuff again like how she was going to be 20 years old & it would have been on Jan 22nd next year & she was about to be 20 in a couple of months' time she would have been 20 in 2000 on Jan 22 20 2000 22 & at school everybody thinking she did mean to do it like in English with horrible Ellis cow looking at me from the front of the class all sympathetic fucking sad eyes like I'm an invalid or freak or something that day we were reading that book Tess of the D'Urbervilles by T Hardy & there is that bit in it where she is looking in the mirror suddenly she thinks that we all know our dates of birth but that every year there is another date that we pass over without knowing what it is but it is just as important it is the other date the death date I could feel everybody in the whole place the boys too all the eyes going into my back & Gemma on the one side & Charlotte on the other not looking because they all knew about it it sent this funny tingling through everything made everything like woah fuck sake weird like something had happened & nobody could say it & I knew I was supposed to be thinking that she had had her other date maybe she had even decided it to do it on it & it was 24 May May 24 & the thing is for once I wasn't actually fucking thinking it or anything about it for once I had been thinking of something else I had been listening to a story about something else a girl looking in a mirror that's all then I had to think about it didn't I because everybody knew & was expecting me to though nobody would fucking well dare say so out loud would they no & then that night &

188

for a long time after it was all I could think about was
how she had had all those 24 Mays one after the other &
on every one of them she must've woken up got up like
usual had her breakfast she used to have just an apple for
her breakfast our mum shouting at her because an apple
isn't enough breakfast for a growing girl breakfast being
the most important meal of the day that she saw in a
magazine or on TV or something she must've been made
to eat other stuff when we were smaller & they could still
make her eat it Frosties or something Rice Krispies I suppose I don't know I don't remember & then she'd have
walked to school not when she was really small of course
like before I was born but after I was born she was nearly
five after that she'd have walked to school primary school
first at Edwards's & then when she was eleven Bourne
Comp on that date 24 May if it was a weekday & probably she went to the pool or whatever on it & now I
know for sure she didn't do it on purpose she didn't know
it was her other date it just was   it is kind of horrible
that idea in that book I can't get it out of my head that
that day is always there & the day comes round I wonder
if I ever feel anything when the date comes round on my
own day I think if it hadn't actually happened in real life
& we had been reading that book at school I would have
thought that it was kind of a cool idea even though it's
in such an old long book with all those boring bits about
fate I can't remember anything else out of it except the
horse getting killed   & the baby   & the man with
the moustache   there was obviously a lot more death

in those days & the blood on the ceiling that was in the film they showed us of it what if I was looking at a ceiling like I am now then I saw blood spreading all over it & it dripped through into the room & fell on to my bed uh that is so horrible because she they didn't tell us he didn't say tonight that man if she did I don't know maybe you don't have to maybe you don't bleed if you just all break up inside but I was thinking about I was thinking about something else yes 24 May the date thing in the book I was thinking yes since with it actually happening in real life it makes it not like cool any more no it's more like you just can't not think about it because what is it like   it is like like reading a book yeah like say you were reading a book any book & you were halfway through it really into the story knowing all about the characters & all the stuff that's happening to them then you turn the next page over & halfway down the page it just goes blank it stops there just aren't any more words on it & you know for sure that when you picked this book up it wasn't like that it was like a normal book & had an end a last chapter a last page all that but now you flick through it right to the end & it's all just blank nothing to tell you   yes that is a bit like what it is like

& since in September he & mum gave it to some friends of the Hendersons the Hendersons had said they knew some people who wanted a single bed suppose they didn't tell the people who have it now that it belonged to someone who was fucking well dead deadbed death bed ha ha

190

wonder who's sleeping in it now wonder what they'd do if
they knew wonder if they'd still sleep in it & now it's my
room not our room they took off the mattress got it out
the door sideways put it on top of a car he dismantled the
slats & wrapped the flex off an old heater round them to
hold them together he couldn't get it to tie in a knot
because of it being rubber they all clattered on to the
pavement the man had to pick them up he put them in the
back of the car it was an estate car the mattress looked
small kind of nothing on the top of it when I looked out
the window I was surprised how small because a bed
seems big when you are quite close up to it but from a bit
further away it is small it looked like just a child's bed
they carried the frame out I could hear them trying to edge
it out the door behind me then it was gone they unscrewed
it put it in the back with the seat down & now there's just
space in here it's like the room is the same but changed
empty too light lopsided or something but there are the
dents left in the carpet they prove it was there if you put
your hand down & feel you can feel the dips where the
feet of the bed were & there was all dust down the back
of it that he hoovered up they told us in Biology that a lot
of dust is made of human skin so if that is true then some
of Sara is in the hoover   God   but she would be
laughing she was always in trouble for not hoovering
behind the bed picked up what I could of it still there after
he hoovered & it is in the handkerchief in with my pants
& tights underneath them in the top drawer because
maybe it came off you Sara it is possible like when your

191

skin peels off in summer maybe I have some of her skin
from spring 1999 in the top drawer   God   fuck
sake one minute there is   & the next you are   you
were just flakes of whatever   stuff   that you can't
even see properly   God   now all of the chest of
drawers is mine though there isn't enough of my stuff yet
I don't have enough they close now before they were all
stuck out stuffed full with stuff & half the wardrobe
empty like she just upped & went ran away from home
my stuff all spread out across the rail to make it look like
nothing was taken but all her stuff was taken away well
he missed the spare overall didn't he yeah but all the
pictures too he took off the wall & they repapered it
because the Blu-tack had left the marks now it is red
stripes but only on the one wall stupid used to be George
Clooney & Carol Hathaway & Pulp & Romeo & Juliet
poster stuck over the old paper God it is really freaky all
those things are already so not what people have on their
walls any more it makes it seem like it happened years ago
instead of like just   then he put the swimming stuff in
the outside dustbin I didn't know he had when I went out
& opened it to put in the onion peel there was all this gold
& silver the medals & statues & the shields & everything
I picked it all out & took it all back inside my arms were
full of her prizes the ones she won when she was small the
ones she won when she was in the inter-school sports all
the Junior Championships the diving one she won last
year it was all smelling like the bin I brought it back into
the livingroom & put it all down on the carpet he went

fucking mad ballistic he was a man needing a lobotomy
put them back outside I'm warning you I won't tell you
twice Clare right now put them back outside well he did
tell me twice didn't he yeah some of the medals had her
name on them as well engraved into their backs I looked
at it all on the livingroom carpet & I said I said something
I can't believe I actually said something out loud I said
yeah but this rosebowl thing has to be passed on next year
to the next person who wins it you can't just throw it
away it's not yours to he went quiet even angrier I could
tell from the breathing he took it in his hands held it like
not to get any marks on it put it on the top of the sideboard opened the sideboard door put it inside closed the
door then got everything else up off the carpet wrapped it
in a teatowel put it back in the dustbin the next day he
took the rosebowl out of the house with him in a carrier
bag when he went to work then going round the house for
days with a look on his face his shoulders hunched up like
the fucking hunchback of wherever hunched up like he's
carrying a backpack full of stuff I don't know what stones
bricks rocks hope it's fucking heavy anyway I can hear
him now that endless fucking snoring I can hear him
turning over in his sleep he has no fucking trouble sleeping does he no he fucking doesn't & our mum   not
our   only my   completely out of it going round
like she's a ghost herself all the time getting that stuff
from the doctor to help her ami or mazi something that
creep Brett from fourth year saying to me is your mother
or father on anything after the funeral and everything

193

bring it in I can sell it for you I told him to fuck off he said
if it's a good dosage I'd get a good price on it fuck off
fucking wanker doesn't matter what they say wankers all
this time it's been ClareWilby'ssister   didherselfin
ClareWilby'ssister   didherselfin those fucking
wankheads at the north gate shouting it when I went past
on the other side of the road & now I know she didn't
now I have proof so they can all fuck off   wait till I
tell mum & dad   but I can't can I I can't just like say
it over the tea things him going off his head because
someone is mentioning it again her not eating anything
not seeing anything not hearing anything all broken in her
chair like someone snapped her off a tree & broke her like
you can break a bit of branch into bits suppose I could say
to her if I got her on her own if he's out or isn't in the
room or is in the bath or fucking shaving again with that
wheeeeeee fucking razor going & can't hear I could tell
her listen it's all right I know it wasn't on purpose for any
reason or anything I know because I went to the place I
went to the hotel I met the people that work there & this
man told me it was by accident for definite he was
actually there he saw it because she was meant to be on
the same shift as him all week & they were talking about
loads of stuff he said they were just having a laugh they
were even going to be going to a film on their night off
they had arranged it Happiness she was just playing
around it was by mistake it wasn't supposed to but I'm
not supposed to ever say fucking anything am I I'm just
supposed to keep out of the fucking way imagine if I

spoke actually said something the walls of this house
would fucking fall down in shock like a ghost had spoke
nobody's supposed to say anything about anything real
how would I say it anyway it's too real to how would I
start if I did what first words would I use what first word
& anyway if I did she'd be too spaced out to hear or the
crying would start that would make him go mad again
it'd be like when he took down the photos or threw out
the swimming stuff all that gold & silver the diving
trophy that's shaped like a dolphin under the ground now
out at the dump dark unless they have streetlights out at
the dump as well do they buried anyway now under the
rubbish all mixed in with old teabags & leftover food
condoms shit with like a skin of mouldy stuff over all of it
like there is on the split binbags dumped for months down
the back of the railway bridge & by now there'll be the
tons of other shit that's been thrown away just since then
as well pressing all her swimming stuff in even deeper into
the ground like buried treasure one day someone will
maybe dig it up like on the programmes where they do
excavating to find out what a society was like in the old
days & it will be like finding something really good under
there & they will have her name on them & people will
wonder who she was in hundreds of years' time centuries
from now they will be in a museum in a glass case &
people looking at them will say I wonder who Sara Wilby
who won the 50 m Butterfly 1996 Junior League all those
hundreds of years ago was I wonder what she was like as
a person & what her life was like she must have been a

very fast swimmer to win but maybe in the future they will think our fast was slow they will all be going so fast themselves God she was fast though she was really really fast we used to go & watch her when they could still make me go & she was always miles ahead reaching the side turning that way under the water like doing a somersault in it pushing off first from the side in one push way ahead miles ahead of whoever she was racing you couldn't believe she could stay under for so long then her shoulders & head bursting up out of it imagine her taking a breath after holding it for so long imagine not being able to breathe & then at the last minute being able to again that would be fucking amazing she always came first in the races where there weren't any good swimmers & at least second or placed in the ones where there were really good swimmers they had to be really good to beat her we were up in the spectator seats him shouting clapping waving his arms in the air then afterwards with the towel round her shoulders the water running down her legs & her shoulders & her neck her hair all sticking up water on her face all over her we were standing at the poolside I remember a friend of mum's saying you should teach your little sister to swim too Sara you'd have two medal-winners in the family everyone laughing & him giving me that look because he knew no way no fucking way was he or any of them ever getting me near fucking water doing that swimming thing in front of everybody everybody thinking it is hilarious because she's this great medal-winner & I can't even swim now when the bits of her start coming by themselves I think of the water running like that down from one part of her to the next & it kind of holds her together to think of water running down her like that it means her head is on her neck & her neck is on her shoulders & her shoulders are on her body with her arms etc the smell of chlorine or whatever they put in the water always in our bedroom always the smell of it kind of faint round her bed & out in the hall too because of the swimsuits in the laundry basket I can still smell it at least I think   far away   no I'm imagining   wonder if her bed still smells of it & the Hendersons' friends are wondering what that is they keep smelling in their bedroom they won't know what it is they won't be able to work it out there was that one night I was still awake & she was falling asleep suddenly she jerked awake again she jerked so fast the bed moved her whole body kind of jolted I said what she said God she laughed she said I was just dreaming I fell off a pavement down the side of a kerb   that was just a couple of weeks before she got killed died God it is amazing what people will do so they don't have to say the word or come anywhere near anyone who has been anywhere near it like at school looking embarrassed like I've done something to embarrass them it's sad no that's not sad sad is what it was when Fluff died that's how I remember it sad looking round & there being no cat in the kitchen or on the chair it was very sad but that was cat-sized sad with this it is as if the kitchen is meaningless it is stupid to even have one the chair is irrelevant it is what is not on it or in it that is made into

everything the only other dead person I really knew is
Granddad & that was so long ago & when he used to sit
in the garden with his chest bare in the sun it was all loose
folds round his neck & face like he was too small for his
skin now it was folding in on him it isn't the same at all as
with her it was like he was getting ready to go like inside
he was too light for a skin that had got too thick & heavy
for him but with her it was perfect hers fitted her perfect it
was all stretched & ready about her about to go a long
way as if she was an arrow or something & all someone
had to do was put her in a bow & shoot her into the air
yeah & all the people at the funeral saying her name
wrong & looking embarrassed neighbours if I meet them
outside or if I'm at the shops & there's someone who
knows mum or him it's this funny sideways look & how
are you all coping a dreadful loss like we lost a purse or a
dog or a terrible way to lose one's life like she just put it
down somewhere & when she looked up she didn't know
what she'd done with it a terrible way to lose someone
close like we lost her in a department store in the sports-
wear dept & if we went to the customer service desk we
could put a call out for her over the intercom speakers
this is a message for Sara Wilby your family is waiting at
customer services could Sara Wilby please come back
from the dead   ah   shit   ah   & so & so
now now she's passed away hasn't she well that's more
like it passed in a fraction of a 0.45 of a fucking second
into the next world the beyond yeah where all the dead
people are standing about smiling Sara & Granddad &

the Grannies with them & Fluff & that old lady from
across the road that died all of them singing someone's
crying lord kum by yah with dead Mrs Kincher from
primary three strumming it on the guitar for them nobody
will say it will they the word dead your sister's dead she
died Mrs Johnstone from up the road stopping me on the
way to school telling me I understand what you are
feeling holding that psycho way on to my arm her eyes all
wide it is a void that no one can fill well I suppose there's
something in that because when I looked inside the shaft
I could see that the steel grooves the things made of steel
or iron that helped the whatever it's called the lift for
food and dishes to go up and down the shaft are all still
there attached to the back of the wall huh they could
pretend easy enough that the lift shaft wasn't there by
putting a piece of wood over it & painting it the same
colour as the wall but they couldn't take the metal off the
wall inside could they no they couldn't be bothered to do
that still there running from the top of it all the way down
to the   bottom of it   & there was a little wheel at
the top inside it for the steel rope that held it the wheel is
still there too about the size of a jaffa cake I reached in &
pushed it it went round smooth as anything like it would
still work like nothing had really changed & God knows
what it would take to fill that cavity Mr Dentist lorry-
loads of fucking concrete but they haven't it is still there it
was just disguised all I had to do was look I saw I looked
down it one minute she was at the top exactly where I was
tonight the next minute   something about that metal

still being there like it would always be there I suppose that even if they did fill it up with concrete in a way even so it would still be there it would still be the same hole just filled with concrete that's all & even if they knocked down the whole of the hotel & that lift shaft was taken apart & wasn't there any more it would still somehow be there though you couldn't see it & didn't know it but that means if that's true then it's also true that because Sara was here because she walked along streets or pulled water towards her like when she used to swim her arms pulled it so she could propel herself through it then somehow she is still here too but that's a lot of shit because she's gone I mean she's really really gone   aren't you   & so if they ever knock down that building or even just its insides say if they were making it into a different building but keeping its outsides they like to do that keep the outer shell of a building & change all the insides like they did with that cinema in Merret St where you were going to see Happiness eventually I suppose they will do that change the building & by then it won't matter that someone fell down it & died because by then no one will remember anyway no one will know

& since it happened there I think that's why I was going & sitting outside it because I didn't know where else to I don't know why I just wanted to know something I don't know what but all there was at home was fucking dents in the carpet fucking nothing just them sitting on stupid chairs staring at the off TV I don't know I don't know what I thought was going to happen did I think you

were going to come back again going to just appear out of
nowhere round a corner waving saying hi thought I was
dead didn't you well no I've been here the whole time
hanging around I've hired a room I live here now had you
all worried didn't I well of course I knew fucking nothing
like that was going to happen & anyway dead people
when they come back aren't like when she came back just
wearing her cardigan like normal usually they're always
vampires or weird & scary moaning on about revenge or
not there at all they just move things round rooms
invisible like with the what are they called   polter-
geists or floating outside the windows like in that film
Salem's Lot those are just stories it wasn't like that you
wouldn't be like that you wouldn't be a vampire with
stupid teeth you would be just yourself but what if she
was herself like she is must be now under the ground her
face all   no no she would just be standing there she
would be wearing her swimming things or her jeans &
pyjama top like at home like she was all the times when I
thought she was standing there then I stopped being able
to do that making her up didn't I fucking lobotomic all
that was left was the bits of her coming by themselves
there has to be some way of stopping them doing it &
then I found the uniform when I put it on it was a bit big
the buttons all the way up the front it must be the spare
the one she wasn't wearing when not the uniform obviously it's not the one because when she fell   it was
just lying there under my coat folded up they must have
missed it when they cleaned the wardrobe out nobody

noticed it because if they had they'd have thrown it out
for sure I hadn't noticed it till now so it was a sign I
thought if I got inside I could find out for sure but then it
was that woman at the front desk who was always
coming out over the road who was on & she'd already
been out tonight I'd already done a runner so I thought
maybe tonight wasn't the best night but then it was after
all when I came back I had it on under my fleece I took
the fleece off at the door I was going to try to slip past
when I got inside like just be a new member of staff so
she wouldn't know or notice but when I went in she was
asleep totally out of it with her head down on the desk I
didn't have to say anything to anybody about why was
I there nobody asked nobody stopped me nobody even
saw me I just walked up the stairs & went up to the top
floor where it had happened I knew it was the top floor it
had happened on it was in all the papers with that school
photo of her from 6th form TALENTED SWIMMER
DEAD   FREAK ACCIDENT CLAIMS LOCAL
GIRL SWIMMER   TRAGIC TEENAGE
DEATH DIVE when I looked them up in the library I
found the hollow place by knocking on the wall   then
later when that woman from the desk Lisa came upstairs
& found me she didn't throw me out or anything she
wasn't angry she said it was a bit of a mess & that she'd
sort it out with the hotel maintenance actually she was
nice I always thought she'd be horrible when she used to
come across the road but she wasn't she had this key in
her pocket that could open any of the doors she knocked

on a door & when there wasn't an answer she opened it
with her key & went in & came back out with kleenex my
nose was really blocked it was quite hard to breathe it can
be quite hard to after you cry I had been really crying I
think it was because of the lift shaft because actually
fucking seeing it it was so dark in there old-smelling the
thing was I couldn't see the bottom of it or how far away
or how near how long it would take or how short I knew
as soon as I saw it all opened up like that I suppose I just
knew that of all the things that were sad about it this was
the saddest that it didn't matter not really whether she
had wanted to do it or not it didn't make any difference
either way just the fact that one minute she'd been there
right there on the exact same spot where I was and the
next she wasn't   & she was holding out the kleenex
now she asked me where my other shoe was I ignored her
she said whose was all that money on the floor I thought
if I just went on ignoring her she would go away but she
said it looked like the wall was a giant slot machine &
that I had hit the jackpot that kind of made me want to
laugh because that was exactly what it looked like like all
that money had come spewing out of the wall or
something she went back into the bedroom & came out
with a wastepaper bin & picked up all the money & told
me I had to go downstairs now with her I thought she
might phone the police I was going to make a run for it
but she had my arm she put me in a back room like an
office with lockers & a kettle kind of place while she
helped someone get their key & answered a phone then

203

she came & got me by the arm & she stood outside this cupboard & knocked on it & the door opened it was full of junk stuff everywhere & a man came out he was like a bear blinking in the light like he'd just been wakened out of a cave he used to know Sara the woman said for me to tell him my name & she told him I needed new shoes & he said what size was I & came back out with a pair of quite old-looking Doc boots with zips up their front in one hand & a newish pair of white ankle Nikes kind of low slung in the other really sleek like they'd hardly been worn at all they really fitted then she came back from behind the desk she had a Dustbuster she told him he had to go & clean up the top floor with it she said did I want to go back up there for a minute too so I asked her could I borrow her watch if it had a hand for seconds it did she gave it to me through the banister when I got up to the top floor the man who used to know Sara was standing staring at the wall like woah fuck sake he said to me did you do this I nodded I thought I was going to get it he sat down like his legs folded under him & he told me the whole story I didn't think I wanted to know it but then it was kind of amazing to know they were watching TV just before & it was a western about some people in the snow with Warren Beatty & someone else in it & then that she bet him a fiver she could get into the lift & she did he saw her in it all folded in upside down he said he was going to say a sentence he was going to say you must be double-jointed because that lift was only big enough for a child of eight but by the time he got half way through the sentence

all there was was the cables whipping out & by the time
he'd got to the end of the sentence there had already been
the noise of it hitting oh God but I knew that stuff about
the upside down already I did because I had read
something about it in the papers so it wasn't that new to
me really he was shaking his head had his hands in his
eyes & when I could hear & think again without that
hum in my ears like something electric like his fucking
wheeeeee razor I hadn't really wanted to know not really
I had only really wanted to do it I went over to the place
I had my other trainer spare I could use I reckoned that
would do it & I had the watch so this time I'd be able to
do everything right I was careful I dropped it down & did
the listening for it & when I looked back he had his hands
out of his eyes now the man he was watching me well I
was fucking well done by then anyway I was nearly off
down the stairs but the man came after me held the door
open with his foot he made this noise in his throat he was
holding something out to me I didn't know what it was it
was grey-blue folded paper kind of scuffed he said this
thing he said we made a bet & I owe it to her so can I give
it to you I think he meant he owed you it Sara I unfolded
it it was a five pound note it had been folded so hard right
down into a square that when I unfolded it it had little
squares all over it when I got down to the ground floor
there was a new person at the desk I thought for a minute
I would get caught & be in trouble about the wall I was
just going to walk out the door like I was a guest the
daughter of a guest or something but that Lisa came from

through the back she took me in there again & she made
me sit down ordered me the breakfast full English it was
on the menu she let me choose it I gave her back the
watch it was half one I'd been up there ages it hadn't felt
like any time at all then she went away & came back with
the breakfast it was huge there were two eggs not one
there was bacon two sausages some round black stuff I
think it was black pudding I don't know there were beans
in a bowl separate from everything else maybe in case
people don't like beans there was loads of toast it was cut
into triangles piles of it on a plate I think she brought
extra everybody had some the new woman at the front
desk took some through on a plate & a man in overalls
came & had some he was really nice to me & the man
from the top floor who knew you he had some too when
he came down & the butter was in these curls in white
dishes there was a choice of jams they were in jars like
actually smaller than my thumb you could get raspberry
or strawberry or apricot or blackcurrant I had raspberry
the breakfast was great it was on the house I couldn't eat
it all people kept saying come on more you can do it it
was really nice people kept patting my back like they
knew me or they'd known me for ages or something
everybody was nice then that Lisa walked me home it was
funny to walk home in the new Nikes the ground felt
different like there was air between me & it she stayed
outside till I shut the door waving goodbye funny for it to
be so good & so sad both at once she said to me on the
way home I looked like I needed sleep I told her I wasn't

sleeping much & she said she was sleeping too much & I could have some of her sleep hours she'd send them to me imagine if you could do that lend someone some hours you weren't using that would be so cool to be able to do that you could put them in an envelope & send them through the post saw-these-hours-&-thought-of-you but it is funny not ha ha but peculiar that it could be so sad I could be there & feel how sad it was then the next minute I could be eating this great breakfast & wearing these great Nikes & feeling really the best in ages it is sort of the same thing as reading the book & the story suddenly stopping because actually though it looked like it had stopped it hadn't it went on & it's all right to be relieved that it did because actually it's okay that it did that it does it's even good kind of like the date thing when everybody in the class was expecting me to be feeling something & for one fucking minute I had forgotten what it was I was supposed to be feeling as if like someone sent me a minute of relief a minute of something else through the post saw-this-minute-&-thought-of-you well it's like tonight started out being about the usual end thing then it changed into something quite different unexpected kind of as if someone somewhere must have seen this evening & thought of me

& since you went quite early on after you went I started making them while I was lying here lists of all the things that you could have been including a swimmer a swimmer obviously but the thing is you could have been anything a doctor someone selling jumpers in a shop selling shoes in a shoe shop papers in a paper shop someone who looked after trees & bushes at a garden centre see all anyone is talking about at school is the millennium this the millennium that what will you do for the millennium five hundred words on how you will make the world a better place in the millennium & all I can think is that the list of things it would have been possible for you to do is never fucking ending it goes on forever new things adding to it all the time you could have been a TV vet or done the things they keep telling us to do at school with computers & personnel or got married or been a person working in a hospital the night a dead girl who'd fallen down a lift shaft got brought in & then like on ER the story would have gone on for you instead of stopping I guess nobody would watch that programme if it just stopped every time someone that got brought in died the story goes on & on for the doctors & nurses every week & on Casualty too even though there are patients that die on them all the time imagine if it stopped just because people stopped there would be nothing but blank screens on the TVs all round the country five minutes after the start of each episode people would be banging the tops of their TVs throwing their remotes across the room there would be riots I am watching TV for you in case you are missing it I am keeping up with Brookside for you it is seriously crap & not just George Clooney is out of ER now but there is a rumour that Carol is going to leave too so you would be pretty pissed off though it is funny to think how you maybe don't know about that when everybody in the

whole wide fucking world knows it & when I eat a piece
of toast it is slowly so I will remember for you what it
tastes like first the burnt taste then the taste where the
butter has melted in & the jam taste like tonight then the
tougher taste when you get to the crust whatever I eat I
eat slowly to see what it really tastes like to eat an orange
or whatever & chicken & a potato in gravy that I know
you liked for instance today at lunch there were frozen
peas they tasted of peas like frozen peas taste do you
remember & one time I stood up on the arm of the couch
when there was nobody else in the room & put my hand
on the top of the door for you where the wood is still kind
of rough up there it isn't painted I don't think it has ever
been painted since whoever built the house there's loads
of like years' worth of dust & stuff is all layered on I think
our whole fucking family is up there in layers including
the cats & when I came down I touched the velvet of
the armcover of the reclining chair so you would know
what it felt like though the touch of velvet makes a shiver
go down my spine like if you scratch your finger across
one of those old vinyl singles in his collection   not
you   me   & I look at things hard so you will
know if you want to what they look like the new cars I saw
on the car transporter coming into town were so new they
didn't have numberplates they were really cool really
smooth-looking they looked really good really fast because
cars are getting faster & I have even been to the pool yeah
the pool me so I can smell it for you too the smell of the
water & the chemical & shampoo smell   the smell is

of you   I went on Tuesday last week in lunchbreak
there were kids splashing this guy dived in he was crap he
hit the water too hard sounded like it was sore yeah I
know believe it or not the pool where I wouldn't have
gone for any money I wouldn't have been seen dead there
ha ha get it listen a dog goes into a bar in the Wild West
right & he goes up to the bar & he says I'm looking for
the man who shot my paw or is that like a stupid little
sister joke & maybe you can hear things like that joke
anyway when it's actually happening maybe you were
listening when Laura told me it at the newsagents I don't
know whether I have to remember them & tell you later
like now I hope it's not boring to hear it over again if you
heard it already did you hear the one about the man who
built a paper shop it blew away I am going fucking mad
talking to a dead person a person who's dead & can't
hear anything & here I am talking to it telling it jokes for
fuck sake I am losing my mind would Clare Wilby's mind
please report to customer services it's me that's the joke I
am such a joke still my heart is going so fast about
something it is racing away ahead of me it is kind of
amazing to talk to her like that amazing because
I talk to her all the time now we never used to talk at all
hardly ever but now all the time I can't get my head round
it if someone is dead they can be more alive than they are
when they're actually like alive that is mad that is
lobotomic it really is I have to not think like that it is
backward it is fucking retarded if anybody knew it was
me who was leaving those sweets there they would put me

in a mental hospital but I don't see what the difference is
it is okay to plant stupid crocuses though I don't know if
she ever even liked crocuses but I do know that she liked
them because she showed me how to suck the sugar dust
off & what the toffee looked like after you did muddy
white she had it between her teeth opened her mouth so I
could see she said there were two different ways to eat it
you could eat it with the sugar still on just chew it really
hard straight away that was one way & one taste then
you could also do the sucking the sugar off thing then
chew it & that was a different taste so I thought they were
as good a thing to leave maybe even better actually since
she stopped getting to eat any of that stuff to slim down
for swimming so she could be faster I can still remember
when she showed me it in her mouth it was all lit up
because of the way it was covered in her saliva that is so
fucking weird I am going weird if anyone knew I thought
these things or went around leaving sweets in cemeteries
for a dead person who can't fucking well exactly eat them
can she I still just don't get it a dead person & her a dead
person & her how the two things are the same thing
where does it go where did she how one minute can you
be walking about & the next you can't as if like you just
got lifted up & disappeared into the sky or you turned a
corner & fell off the side of the world & nobody can
phone you or anything & I saw what happened to that
mouse that we put in the shed after Fluff got it it wasn't
bleeding but it was in shock that's what mum said we put
it on the saucer & put another saucer with water near it

211

but when we got back from the holiday & opened the
shed door there weren't even any bones left just a swarm
of white things moving back & fore on the saucer we
threw it away the whole thing the saucer too   & also
& also there are all these rules like when Teresa Drewe
her family's Catholic she went to a Catholic school before
Bourne's she came up to me at art when we were doing
the time capsules & told me about how saints actually get
to be saints because they have had to endure these painful
deaths so maybe it was good to go like that she said but
then she said was it true that it was on purpose because
that meant that she couldn't get into heaven & that
wherever she was buried it would turn the ground into
unconcentrated ground well it wasn't on purpose was it
& that thing about how there are even people who carry
bits of dead saint around with them to keep safe or
blessed or whatever it is it's kind of like people who have
those real white rabbits' paws on their keyrings for good
luck like Uncle Martin showed us that time with the claws
of the rabbit still in it well I suppose the handkerchief in
the drawer the handkerchief in the drawer is kind of like
that maybe though I don't want to not have it I like
knowing it's there certainly wouldn't tell anybody about
it or show anybody because they would think it was so
disgusting & lobotomic but Sara I know Sara would
laugh she would laugh about the hoover if she was here
then I would make a joke about how she is so light now
how she is so not heavy any more that she could easy
shave 0.45 off her butterfly in fact she could easy be the

fastest swimmer in the whole fucking world if she wanted
to if that's what she wanted to be she's so light now she
could be fast as the wind fast as fucking light I would say
it & she would hit me over the top of my head that stern
look on her face her hand scuffing the top of my hair like
it was a stupid little sister thing & I wonder if I maybe
looked a bit like her when I had the uniform on we don't
really didn't really look alike but maybe a little bit I must
have looked a bit like her I must have looked a bit

   & since the bits of her all broken apart still aren't
coming haven't come tonight yet yet thank God thank
fuck it is not them but my heart going so fast that's
keeping me awake yeah along with the fucking noise of
him through there still snoring I can't believe anyone
could snore so much & not wake up he's a heavy sleeper
ha that is the fucking understatement of the year of the
century of the millennium it sounds like someone drilling
bricks out of the side of the house someone mowing the
carpet with one of those lawn-mowers that you push that
don't have a motor except it sounds as loud as louder
than a motor it is no fucking wonder I never fucking sleep
haven't slept properly for months I wonder if that Lisa
will send me some of her sleep hours that was nice I don't
remember him snoring like that before it either he's
snoring or he's getting up he'll be getting up in a minute
it'll be that fucking wheeeeeee in a minute morning again
he is always in there these days going at his face with the
razor about three times a day I don't remember really
what it was like before it must have been different from

this I think he thinks I am insolent all the time not just
because I don't say anything but because I am the one
who is still here   & also I know this is true that if I
was thrown into a pool & they would have to throw me
because there is no way I would do the jumping or the
diving in that she could do no way never so if they would
throw me in I would sink straight down & it would be so
embarrassing someone the pool guard probably would
have to dive in & rescue me off the bottom like I was one
of those bricks people practise with sometimes I wouldn't
mind being just an ear just an eye an eyebrow just one
single eyelash blown away like someone held me at the tip
of their finger & made a wish on me blew me away light
as a really really small piece of I don't know uh leaf it
would be a relief to be just that not this with all its feet &
hands & mind going all the time Sara you are lucky oh
God   what am God no I don't mean it Sara I didn't
mean anything by it I didn't   she had the most
fucking amazing eyelashes they were so long longer than
anybody else's I will ever know & there they were just on
the ends of your eyelids going down & up whenever you
closed your eyes & opened them or blinked just blinked
like we all do thousands of times a day where did they go
your eyelashes were they hurt a thing happened on
Saturday when I went to Sainsbury's with mum she sat by
the door while I paid at the till they gave me the change &
the receipt I was scrunching it up to put it in my pocket &
I noticed it said right at the bottom of it the words
goodbye hope to see you again & I was walking back over

214

to mum she was sitting near the newspapers & it came
into my head from nowhere I remembered that night quite
near the end when I was getting ready for bed & you were
in your bed you were looking at me I could see your eyes
in the dark you were just looking at me nothing else just
the looking it was I don't know suddenly terrible my
whole insides filled it made me angry it was sore it filled
me up as simply as water will fill a cup a sink a bath a
pool a river the ocean basin or whatever you put it in it
filled me so I could hardly breathe came right up over my
nose like I was too small for the depth of it Sara do you
remember you had a pain in your stomach one day in that
week you first went to work at the hotel & do you
remember you took that pink stuff that comes in the
bottle with the plastic cup on the top of it well inside the
bedside cabinet your cabinet from the side of your bed I
went through it before they took it away I found the cup
it was the week after you & there was a little of the pink
stuff left at the bottom that you hadn't drunk it had
solidified inside the cup I picked it out with the tips of my
nails it was exactly the shape of the inside of the cup &
even had printed on it the writing from off the bottom of
the cup except backwards that is amazing isn't it it is
interesting eh it is inside my cabinet at the back now I am
going to keep it for as long as it keeps for I don't know if
it will last it is kind of papery-feeling now it has darkened
in colour it doesn't smell of anything but I touched it with
my tongue it tastes sort of sweet it is lobotomic I know
but I couldn't not keep it in a way it is kind of like the five

215

pounds he owed you I put the five pounds in the cabinet
too I won't ever spend it it is yours in a way it means you
maybe because it means you it will call you back or if you
know it is here you will come back for it it belongs to you
even if you don't I will keep it for you it is worth more
than anything I have flattened it out between two books
Linda Goodman's Sun Signs & your dictionary you had
from school it is full of words you could have looked up I
am always wondering when I look at it which of the
words you needed to know the meanings of it is funny
how many words there are & nothing ever even said it is
as if I've thought so many fucking words out into this
room not ours mine by now that I am swimming in them
ha sinking more like they must be like several metres deep
now maybe this bed is afloat on them like a ship a rowing
boat no maybe I'm already under them & breathing like a
fish through gills I didn't know I had maybe I am a better
swimmer than I thought here I go swimming swooping
about who needs oxygen I am a great fucking swimmer
God staying awake so late is better than drugs any time
now I am swimming about on the deck of a boat & the
boat is under what is the word for deep water under deep
miles of all these words I haven't said I wonder if words
are light or heavy I suppose it depends what they're saying
or what they're not saying well dictionaries though are
hardly fucking light are they oh I think that was a bird
was it there is always one bird starts the whole fucking
raft of them off cheeping not long till the morning comes
up till morning has broken like the first morning like that

216

hymn from school blackbird has spoken etc spoken ha ha
more like fucking yelling it IT'S MORNING AGAIN
EVERYBODY UP COME ON EVERYBODY
WAKE UP when I was small I used to think that the
day break would be the same as switching on a light in a
dark room but really in actuality the light is grey hardly
like light at all more like the going away of light I think
the most fucking amazing morning I ever saw was when
there was that low mist the light came up like usual but
I couldn't see anything just mist as if a block of light
nobody could see through was wedged between the
window & the rest of the world as though outside wasn't
there any more & as the day came up the mist moved I
saw it move like a curtain across the garden like something was sweeping it back it was amazing to watch the
world come back   God   that terrible night it
first went away it was early much earlier than it is now
first the phone going it woke me then the knocking on
the door & I got up I was standing at our bedroom door
& they were in the hall already there was the policeman
& the policewoman dad was already dressed but his
pyjama trousers top was coming out of the waistband
of his work trousers then mum was flat against the wall
the policeman standing next to dad with his helmet
under his arm dad looked small beside him like he'd
hurt his back then my heart was falling I felt it something
happened the house had changed something had come
in the door & changed it it wasn't just our house it was
everything outside too like it had all been smashed then

217

stuck together with glue by someone but all in the wrong order & we were standing in the hall at home it had got light outside by itself nobody in the hall moving up it came anyway same as usual the fucking light of day

& since it has been good since then to have some reasons for it & for getting up & breakfast & more of the same & another day again

& since breakfast can actually I forgot taste & smell like really good

& since Sara you used to smell of specially cleaned water & since now you are nothing but air you are not even air any more I don't know what you are

& since when you used to set the table after we got home from school you used to hit the sideboard with the sides of the knives along to whatever was playing on the radio or whatever was on the TV

& since I have the photo of us at Christmas time last year it is in the cabinet under the dictionary he won't find it there neither of them will so she won't be upset by it either it is okay to have it

& since you would laugh about the hoover & the handkerchief thing & the pink stuff in the cup I know you would

& since there was that day when you pulled my hair really hard

& since you got into real trouble when mum brushed my hair & it all came out in a big clump on the brush

& since it hasn't ever grown back properly there since then

& since you could swear better than anybody

& since you covered my arm in bruises after I told
about you swearing

& since I went to Bourne's on my first day in my new
blazer & all those girls from your year your friends
crowded round me at the south gate saying was I your
little sister I don't know if you knew they did that

& since I will always know off by heart I will not forget
the sound of you breathing in the dark

& since there was the night when I was eleven when
they played the old song about the long and winding
road on the radio & for some reason I don't know why
it made me frightened that the earth was full of dead
people even the earth round the flowers outside in the
garden though I didn't say anything I was in bed you
were in the other bed you said what's wrong are you
scared you knew I was without me having to say anything you went through to the kitchen & made toast &
brought it through & climbed in we ate it I fell asleep on
you I woke up the next morning & the plate was still on
the bed on the blankets the crumbs on it so that proved
it happened

& since you could hold your breath for so long under
water

& since you could walk on it water I mean because
there was the time there was almost nobody else in the
pool I was up in the spectator gallery you were below me
you were treading water at the deep end I was amazed I
remember wondering how come she can do that stay on

219

the surface of the deep water like that as if she is just
running on the spot how come she can float like that on
nothing

   & since maybe now you can walk on air too

   & since wherever you are now I know you will be
keeping us me & mum & dad safe

   & since you were there you were definitely there all
those times at the pool I saw you I can see you now up
there on the top board high up much higher than the
spectator seats so we were all looking up at you looking
down at the water there's always the moment before you
jump when you wait just for a split second it looks like
you might not do the dive you can back out of it if you
want as if so what who needs to do it & then all the same
you always did it you stepped forward sent the board
down then up down then up your arms out & you were
off into the air falling it was always so fucking brilliant
you would flash easy through the air like the air was
stretched out beautiful like I don't know what like a fish
like a hot knife through butter like you just diving as
usual into water

   & since in the end when you went & you went with
legs & arms all I know I know upside down stuck in I
know & then it was all over all of it the broken tops of
all the waters over & done with still listen Sara even
though you couldn't even though you couldn't move
couldn't do anything about it listen to me you were fast
you were really really fast I know because I went there to
see tonight I was there & you were so fast I still can't

believe how fast you were less than four seconds just under four three & a bit that's all you took I know I counted for you

present

Morning.

The garden is wet after last night's rain. Winter, with more winter to come; the place is shabby already with the leftovers of the year and it will be three more months before everything dies down and spring can begin to be seen.

The tree is hung with yellows and reds, small inedible apples clawed or dropped. Either way, on the tree or on the ground, they're for the frost. There are leaves left on the branches but the new leaves behind them, sealed shut inside, are inching them steadily off. The lilac is bare. The rhubarb has furled up and gone underground. Two of its huge summer leaves, left over the lawn-mower to protect it from rain, are stuck and rotting on the metal of the blades and frame. The new grass looks singed where the cold scuffed across it. The forsythia is a straggle of dead sticks. But the cranesbill is still flowering. The marigolds are flowering. The daisies and the campanula are finally flowering. The rock rose hasn't stopped flowering. There are little flies suspended in the air, new and reckless. The feverfew is green. The snow-in-summer is green. The strawberry patch is still producing the occasional green strawberry under the leaves at the edge even this late in the year. The birds pick at them if they find them; there are still plenty birds in the sky, the garden, the gradual revelation of branches.

Morning. Already some of the ghosts are out and about.

A Marks and Spencer carrier bag snagged by the wind on a fence can call the ghosts of a thousand middle-aged ladies back to linger by the jumpers and cardigans once more, wandering the aisles and fashions of the not-yet-open store, yearning to finger the wool of the sleeves of the new winter lines if only they could, to hold clothes up against them again and to smell the scent of the new, with the ghosts of their husbands waiting by the door, arms folded, bored, eternally impatient.

High in the north on a street in a town in the misty, cold-bound Highlands, the ghost of Mrs M. Reid is back in front of what used to be her shop, where she sold sugar-sticks and humbugs, gums and liquorices, peppermints, lozenges, chocolate moulded into shapes, new factory-made sweets, fudges she made on the premises herself at the back where there's now a square of tarmac for a car park. So many tooth-rotting things displayed in jars and sold here to so many people for so many years; the bagging them, weighing them, wrapping them, taking the money. Yesterday two men broke the shop sign off the front above Keiths' the Stationer, because Keiths' the Stationer is getting a newly designed sign, and underneath on the shop front the original sign is still there and this is what it says, what it's said under there for seventeen

years, what it's said in the dark under all the other signs
for over a century since Mrs Reid had it painted and
opened her shop after the death of her husband, a man
who had forbidden her to open a shop because it would
embarrass him, a man she hadn't much liked, a man
about whom the people of the town, sucking her peppermints in the Free Church on a Sunday, discussed the
rumour they'd confected that she did it herself, with hot
chocolate made the foreign way by melting down squares
of it over the heat and adding poison for rats; none of
which concerns her now, stately and *fin de siècle* written
up in paint that hasn't faded, back above her place of
business for the light of one more day: Confectioner
~Prop. ~ Mrs M. Reid.

Down the country and over the border, speeding away
from the massed northern ranks of the ghosts of centuries'
worth of anger-wakened warriors baring their wounds
and waving their warty shields, the ghost of Diana,
Princess of Wales, historic and royal ghost, ghost of a
rose, ghost in a million stammering living rooms, ghost
again today on the pages of this morning's *Daily Mail*,
still selling its copies by breathing her back to a life that's
slightly more dated each time, is smiling shy and sweet,
as a girl, in a tiara, in a hacking jacket, holding a baby,
holding a bunch of flowers, looking off to the side in a
fetchingly modest way, waving from a carriage; in a
few hours' time, with the morning well underway,
she will float, merciful, eyes full of sorrow, above all
the squeaky postcard racks of the newsagents and

post offices, above all the teatowels and cups and trays and coasters graced by her graceful full-of-grace face in the many souvenir shops of turn-of-the-century England.

Low in the south in the hazy city the faded shade of Solomon Pavy, child actor who died aged *scarse thirteene* nearly four hundred years ago in the summer of 1602, resentfully woken and set loose again every time someone reads the poem written to his memory by Ben Jonson, who knew him when he was a Child of the Queen's Revels, is loitering in the reconstructed Globe Theatre, quite like it was, though not near good or dirty enough. The mere idea of him roams about backstage, and up in the gallery and balcony. The theatre is closed for the season. It's too early for visitors to the restaurant or the carpeted corporate foyer. This year here there were many plays on by many different writers of the Renaissance, though Solomon Pavy himself (in the teeth of the mournful poem by Jonson which robbed him of proper and soothing oblivion) chose to favour Will, who wrote the Errors before his birth, the killing of Caesar when he was living, and Cleopatra after his death, to his eternal regret, the boy who only ever got to play old men, who never got to know what a Juliet he'd have made had he seen his salad days, but Juliet go hang for what a Cleopatra – oh happy horse, to bear the weight of Antony – as high-voiced and silent he crosses the wooden stage, out into the barren crowdless space, over the wall in a single vault to hover by the river above the heads of the people up early for work or the people coming home from work who traipse the side of it on the brand-new walkway. And further along the line of the river, murky and continuing, out at the site of the Millennium Dome, historic monument to the temporary whose belled-up insides are filled with panic, bluster, rhetoric and air as the new year edges nearer, the fall of a rope from the roof to the floor calls them back for a moment, the choked ghosts who fell to their deaths on the gibbet that stood there before any Dome did, who swing back and fore past the sleepy nightwatchmen, through wired-up security gates, surveillance cameras recording them, absent.

Anywhere up or down the country, any town (for neatness' sake let's say the town where the heft and the scant of this book have been so tenuously anchored) the ghost of Dusty Springfield, popular singer of the nineteen sixties, soars, sure and broken, definite and tentative, through the open window of a terraced house on the corner of Short Street. Over the streets she goes, and the gardens, the spread of estates and the dump, and the black canal with its fetid banks and the swimming pool and the hotel with its pristine and rumpled rooms and up into the sky, dwindling down into town in a voice so faint now it's lost, it can't be heard. Which doesn't mean to say it isn't there; back in Short Street there's no mistaking The Look Of Love, it's in your eyes, a look your heart can't disguise; her hair is high on her head and she is kohl-eyed, young, she moves her arms as if she's holding something close to her, then as if it's flung or flown away; a look that's

229

saying so much more than just words can ever say; a look that time can't erase; she tells everybody who listens, anybody who can hear, that she has waited, how long she has waited, and the neighbours on and round Short Street, who are woken most work-day mornings at seven by the volume of it coming out of 14 Short Street, are lying in bed with pillows over their ears and their heads, scowling into too-early coffee made too fast or weak or strong, shouting abuse at the walls of the bedroom, ringing to leave another message on the council helpline, looking in anger out of the window or the open door in the direction of the noise, grimly listening through it to the eight o'clock news on Radio 4, having details taken down again by the man about to go off shift at the reception desk of the police station, crossing the road so as to knock on the door of number 14 Short Street and, if he or she has the decency to answer the door, to threaten the person with a beating, again, sleeping through it regardless, or listening, even joining in, with the ghost of Dusty who's nearly done now, whose song is in its last fragile cheap crescendo, as she sings *don't ever go*, as the three minutes thirty seconds of song (and behind it all the two-minute, three-minute songs there have ever been about the comings and goings, the gains and the losses, the endless spinning cycles of love and the trivia of living) come, as if on the spread grey wings of common collared-doves descending above a garden to land on the still-wet branches of the crab-apple tree, smoothly, inexorably, down to their close.

*

Morning. The lady who cleans the steps every morning, and the paving outside with the word *Global* tiled into it, has emptied her bucket and put it away with the mop in the store cupboard. She has gone home, hours ago. The word *Global* is still clean; not many people have walked over it yet.

The checkout girls who work in the supermarket are eating breakfast in their work clothes in houses all over town (except for the girls who are part-time, and those whose day off it is, many of whom are still sleeping in beds or making breakfasts for children and men).

The people who bought prescriptions in Boots the Chemist yesterday are feeling better, worse or the same. Some have colds. Some have infections. Some have nothing wrong with them. Some feel drowsy and ought not to operate machinery today. Some have temperatures going up or coming down. Some have healed in their sleep and will wake up refreshed. Some have found, or will find when they wake up, that taking medicine has made no difference at all to how they feel.

The people who queued outside the cinema to see a film yesterday are either awake or asleep. A small percentage of them remembers seeing the film at all.

The driving instructor is drinking Horlicks for breakfast; caffeine makes her jumpy. She is thinking of the feel of the learner driver up inside her. Her husband is having trouble with his tie. She is smiling and answering the questions he asks her, thinking of the feel of the push of the boy up amongst her clothes in the car.

The learner driver is awake in bed going over the lessons he's had so far. Is she a good teacher? his mother asked him last night (his mother is paying for the lessons). Yes, he said. He blushed. She's a really good teacher, he said, she says I soon won't need dual controls and that with the right number of lessons I will easily pass. He has ten more lessons lined up. He is wondering what else he will learn.

The woman who runs the café is waiting in the quiet that comes before the rush every morning. She has made herself a bacon sandwich and is reading today's paper. It is about unnatural perverts again; it isn't as good a story as yesterday's, about the people eaten by sharks. But it raises her moral certitude, which makes her feel cleansed.

The man whose son drove off yesterday, leaving him waving on the pavement, is looking out of the back window into his garden. He has put up bags of nuts on the tree for the birds. The winter birds delight him. There's a chaffinch. There's another chaffinch.

The man who was angry at the lovers pawing each other at the bus stop yesterday is asking his wife to help him fix his tie. Come here, she says, and takes it out of his hands and threads it round his collar and back into itself, over, under, tightened, down. She kisses his cheek. He goes through to the hall and looks in the mirror; he is angry, though he can't think why. He opens the front door, shouts goodbye.

The lovers drunk at the bus stop yesterday are in bed.

He is trying to sleep a little longer, but his hangover hammers his eyes open whenever he closes them. She is awake, tapping ash from a cigarette into a cup. She smiles down at him; bleary, he smiles back.

The builder is sitting on a plank sticking out of a loft extension three storeys up in the air. He is about to wake any people still asleep in the nearby houses with his drill. It is time they were up anyway. Someone, a girl, goes past on a bike. He waves down to her. He doesn't know her. She doesn't know him. She waves back. Morning, love, he calls. He is cheered up. He puts his drill down, looks out over the neighbourhood and begins to whistle the tune of a song he knew when he was a boy.

The woman who was struggling along the road yesterday opens one of the awkward things she was carrying then. It is a plastic container of orange juice as big as her upper body. The more you buy, the cheaper it is. She balances its weight against herself and fills four glasses. She puts them on the kitchen table, one in front of each child.

The woman too large to fit into the swimming pool cubicle is on her bed. She is reading a book and eating a banana. Her cat has made a nest for itself in the folds of her stomach. It has spent the last quarter of an hour grooming and cleaning and is now purring up at her with eyes full of love.

The girl who works in the watch shop is just out of the shower, dry now, sitting on the end of her bed. Her hair is all over her face. She shoves it back behind her ears. She

233

straps her watch to her wrist. It is not her watch. It
belongs to someone else, a customer. A girl came in with
it in the summer and hasn't been back to collect it yet. It is
a really nice watch; there are hundreds like it, all made the
same, but this one's strap has been softened by being
worn so that the feel of it is warm, and it's keeping good
time since it was mended. When she does come back to
ask for it, the girl who works behind the counter is ready
to say, Hello, here it is. I was wondering when you'd be
back for it. I didn't think you'd give up on it. It's a really
nice watch. She won't mind, the girl thinks every morning
when she puts the watch on. *S. Wilby*, it said on the
packet in the filing drawer; the girl checked through the
files for it when Mr Michaels was away at the sales
conference, and found it and opened it, took it out and
looked at it. For weeks on end the watch had been shut in
a drawer of mended watches, all sealed in separate
packets and ticking away to themselves. *S. Wilby. £27.90.*
Water in the mechanism. Twenty-eight pounds; quite a
hefty charge for a watch like this one. She put a line
through it in the file-book and wrote the word *default*
next to it, cancelled it on the computer, folded the invoice
up and put it in her pocket. She took her own watch off.
She slung this other watch round her wrist. The buckle
slid into its usual groove. She and S. Wilby have similar-
sized wrists.

The girl who works in the watch shop has never done
this with anyone else's watch. She is surprised at herself.
S. Wilby stood outside the shop, for days, shy and slight,

undemanding, intriguing, looking down at her feet all the time. She had pretended not to notice S. Wilby. She doesn't know why she did that. It seemed the thing to do. She wasn't ready. The timing was wrong. It was embarrassing. It's embarrassing now, when she thinks about it, and when she does she can feel small wings moving against the inside of her chest, or something in there anyway, turning, tightened, working.

The girl who works in the watch shop has looked up all the Wilbys in the local phone directory and written down their numbers. One day she is going to have guts enough to call them up one after the other and ask whoever answers if there is an S. Wilby at this number whose watch is still waiting to be collected.

In the kitchen she pours cereal into a bowl, then milk. Her mother is at work. Her brother isn't up yet. She gets a spoon from the draining board. She checks the face of the watch. Nearly eight. She will have to walk to work, he isn't up. She will leave in quarter of an hour so as not to be late.

Every morning she thinks it as she fastens the watch on. It is today. She will put her bare wrists on the counter and say, I've come to pick up a watch, for Wilby. The girl in the watch shop will show her the watch on her own arm. I hope you don't mind, she will say. I kind of took a fancy to it.

She finishes her breakfast, glances down at the watch. She'll go in five minutes. She gazes out of the window into the garden.

Look, it's keeping good time, she is planning to say.
And listen, no charge. It's on me.

Morning. One bird lands, then another. The tree shakes
slightly. Rainwater jolts off the branches and falls, a
miniature parody of rain.

remember
you
must
live

remember
you
most
love

remainder
you
mist
leaf

WOooooo-
hooooooo
oo
o

refresh yourself at penguin.co.uk

Visit penguin.co.uk for exclusive information and interviews with
bestselling authors, fantastic give-aways and the
inside track on all our books, from the Penguin Classics
to the latest bestsellers.

BE FIRST

first chapters, first editions, first novels

EXCLUSIVES

author chats, video interviews, biographies, special
features

EVERYONE'S A WINNER

give-aways, competitions, quizzes, ecards

READERS GROUPS

exciting features to support existing groups and
create new ones

NEWS

author events, bestsellers, awards, what's new

EBOOKS

books that click – download an ePenguin today

BROWSE AND BUY

thousands of books to investigate – search, try
and buy the perfect gift online – or treat yourself!

ABOUT US

job vacancies, advice for writers and company
history

Get Closer To Penguin . . . www.penguin.co.uk